ENDORSEMENTS

"A delightful story you'll not want to put down until you finish it. You will turn each page and wonder what will happen next. Naomi Miller is a talented and wonderful author, and I can't wait to read more of her stories."

~ Molly Morris Jebber, author of
Two Suitors for Anna

"A delicious and delightful story with a large helping of fun and a dash of romance."

~ Jennifer Beckstrand, award-winning author of
the *Matchmakers of Huckleberry Hill* series

"I'm ready to pull up a chair in The Sweet Shop, savor a slice of cinnamon bread, and dig into this juicy mystery."

~ Dana Mentink – multi published,
award-winning author

"A sweet, refreshing novella that will satisfy your sweet tooth as you weave your way through the crumbs to find the *"whodunit"*."

~ Goodreads Reviewer

"*Blueberry Cupcake Mystery*" is a warm and cozy mystery just right for reading in one sitting. This short novella is sweet in more ways than one and will not only whet your appetite for a bit of mystery but might just tempt your taste buds with its descriptions of The Sweet Shop's offerings."

~ Vine Voice

"A light-hearted, quick read that will help you escape from the stresses and drama of day-to-day life. Fans of Amish fiction of any age will love this book."

~ Reviewer

"A sweet, fun and intriguing mystery you can really sink your teeth into."

~ Rachel L Miller - author of the Amish romance series: *Windy Gap Wishes*

PUMPKIN

PIE

MYSTERY

BOOKS BY NAOMI MILLER

AMISH SWEET SHOP MYSTERY

BLUEBERRY CUPCAKE MYSTERY

CHRISTMAS COOKIE MYSTERY

LEMON TART MYSTERY

PUMPKIN PIE MYSTERY

CHOCOLATE TRUFFLE MYSTERY

PEACH COBBLER MYSTERY

SOPHIE FINDS A FAMILY

SOPHIE CELEBRATES THANKSGIVING

SOPHIE'S NEW HOME

WITH RACHEL L MILLER

A MOTHER FOR LEAH

A SUITOR FOR REBEKAH

WITH RUTH MILLER

ASHES TO AMISH

HER BEASTLY BLESSING

PUMPKIN PIE MYSTERY

BY

NAOMI MILLER

Pumpkin Pie Mystery
Copyright © 2017 by Naomi Miller

Christmas Cookie Mystery / Naomi Miller

ISBN: 978-1948733175   (Hardbound)
ISBN: 978-0998169255   (Paperback)
ASIN: B01LVW9MHD

1. Fiction / Religion & Spirituality / Christian Books & Bibles / Christian Fiction. 2. Fiction / Mystery, Thriller & Suspense / Mystery / Cozy. 3. Fiction / Christian Books & Bibles / Literature & Fiction / Amish & Mennonite.

LOC

S&G Publishing, Knoxville, TN
www.sgpublish.com

All rights reserved. No part of this publication may be reproduced or transmitted for commercial purposes, without written permission of the publisher, except for brief quotations in printed reviews. Scripture quotations are from the Holy Bible (KJV)

THIS BOOK IS A WORK OF FICTION. NAMES, CHARACTERS, PLACES, AND INCIDENTS ARE EITHER PRODUCTS OF THE AUTHOR'S IMAGINATION OR USED FICTITIOUSLY. ANY SIMILARITY TO ACTUAL PEOPLE, ORGANIZATIONS, AND/OR EVENTS IS PURELY COINCIDENTAL

COVER, GRAPHICS AND FORMATTING BY EXPRESSO DESIGNS
SECOND EDITION 2020

To God be the Glory...

A NOTE FROM NAOMI MILLER

When I felt the Lord calling me to write Amish fiction that was fun to read, free from stress, anxiety, and other stomach-tightening reactions, I wasn't certain if readers would enjoy it. I'm thrilled to find loyal readers who look forward to the release of new books in the series... many more readers than I expected.

As with any work of fiction, I've taken license in some areas of research as a means of creating circumstances necessary to my characters or plot. I've created fictional characters in a fictional town. Any inaccuracies in the Amish, Mennonite or English lifestyles portrayed in this book are completely due to fictional license.

God bless you!

~Naomi

GLOSSARY

The German/Dutch dialect spoken by the Amish
is not a written language. It is solely dependent
on the location and origin of each settlement.
The spellings below are approximations.

ach = oh

aenti = aunt

allrecht = all right

appeditlich = delicious

bruder/bruders = brother/brothers

buwe/buwes = boy/boys

danki = thank you

dat = dad

dochder = daughter

du bischt daheem = you're home

Englischer = non-Amish person

freind/freinden = friend/friends

frau = wife

froh = happy

Gott = God

gudemariye = good morning

gut = good

hochmut = pride

hungrich = hungry

in lieb = in love

jah = yes

kaffe = coffee

kinner = children

kumme = come

maedel/maedels = girl/girls

mamm = mom

naerfich = *nervous*

nee = no

onkel = uncle

rumschpringe = running around time for youth

schweschder/schweschders = sister/sisters

verrickt = crazy

was iss letz = what's wrong

wunderbaar = wonderful

To every thing there is a season...

Ecclesiastes 3:1

For Gwen

ONE

Katie looked across the table at her *freinden*. Freida was giggling as Thomas brushed icing off the end of his nose, a half-smile on his face.

Danki, Gott, for bringing mei two freinden together. They are such a wunderbaar couple.

Katie wondered how she could have missed Freida's true feelings all this time. They had been freinden for many years—ever since they started school together.

However did she keep it from me, her best freind! Why did she never confide in me?

Of course, it had been a surprise for everyone. Katie had not been the only one who thought Freida was interested, not in Thomas, but in his outgoing and high-spirited *bruder*.

Timothy's personality simply seemed more suited to Freida's lively and gregarious nature. Everyone had naturally assumed that he would be courting Freida soon.

Thinking of Timothy and Freida together, Katie could see where she had missed an most important piece of the puzzle.

Katie had always figured that Timothy was somehow missing Freida's attention. Perhaps it was simply because he was too interested in getting into mischief than paying attention to *maedels*.

Fortunately, Timothy's oblivion had worked in everyone's favor. He had paid no attention to Freida, which had given his *bruder* the courage to take the next step.

It had been a surprise to the whole community when the bishop had read the banns for Thomas and Frieda.

Freida's giggles slowly quieted as Thomas took her hand. A look passed between them that sent a feeling of longing through Katie.

Determined to ignore her sudden melancholy, Katie turned her thoughts to other things. The wedding was less than two weeks away—the day before Thanksgiving—and there was much to be done if they were to be ready on time.

Once Freida and Thomas decided on a cake, she would need to check the supplies to make certain she had everything she would need.

She and Freida would need to finish their work on their dresses and aprons. And Katie needed to finish her own work on the quilt she would be giving them for a wedding gift.

Perhaps I could ask mamm to help me with it. She is so much faster at quilting than me. Her stitches are prettier than mine, too.

"Thomas, don't." Freida's words pulled Katie out of her thoughts.

"Nonsense. I am only following your example, dear heart." Thomas said, laughing as he reached toward Freida with a finger liberally covered in frosting.

Freida pulled away, giggling when Thomas smeared the frosting on her nose.

Katie watched her *freinden* laughing over the frosting and cake bits. It was difficult to believe that only a few months ago, Freida had been certain she would never get a proposal from the *buwe* she liked.

To see the two of them today, it would appear that they had been together for years.

And in just over a week, they will be getting married.

A small ache spread through Katie's chest and she was surprised to find herself wiping a tear from her eye.

When Thomas leaned in to wipe the frosting off Freida's nose and place a kiss where it had been, Katie eased her chair away from the table. Neither of her *freinden* seemed to notice as Katie made her way quietly to the kitchen.

For sure and for certain, Freida will let me know which cake they decide on, just as soon as she can.

Katie brushed away several more tears as she went to work, pulling random ingredients off the kitchen shelves and lining them up beside the mixing bowl already sitting on top of the tall, metal prep table.

Working with no real aim in mind, Katie measured ingredients into the bowl, stirring wet into dry, whipping eggs in a separate bowl before adding them to the mixture.

Every few minutes, a laugh floated back to her from the front of the store. She had to remind herself more than once that she was *froh* for her two *freinden*, as she continued to mix and stir, before rolling out dough. Finally, she stopped working, bowing her head before closing her eyes.

Help me, Gott, to be froh for my freinden.

Freida pushed through the swinging doors between the store and the kitchen, with Travis close behind her, just as Katie pulled a tray of cookies from the oven.

"Katie, those look *wunderbaar*. What recipe is that?"

The sweetness and wonder in Freida's voice immediately sent a wave of guilt crashing through Katie.

She had *kumme* into the kitchen to hide from her *freinden* and feel sorry for herself. Because of her own actions, she had most likely missed a lot of the planning and decision-making—plans she should have been involved in, since she was Freida's side sitter.

Turning away to hide the blush that colored her cheeks, she made a show of sliding the cookies onto a cooling rack.

"They are a new recipe, Freida. Nothing special." She waved away her *freind's* praise as the blush spread and filled her face with heat.

"Oh, come on now, Katie. Your recipes are always special. You have to know that." Travis spoke up then, only adding to Katie's embarrassment.

She ducked her head, determined not to say anything else. After all, what could she say? She certainly shouldn't agree with her *freinden* that her recipes were special. *Hochmut* was a difficult, but necessary, thing to avoid.

After several long seconds of silence, Travis spoke again, this time addressing Freida.

"So, did you and Thomas pick a cake, then?"

When Freida answered, her voice was full

of excitement and another emotion that was not easy to identify.

"*Jah*, we did. And I can tell you it was no easy thing, with how *wunderbaar* Katie makes everything taste." She laughed, then Katie heard her footsteps moving away.

Katie sniffed, blinking away the tears that unexpectedly attempted to escape—tears she thought she had gotten control over. And then, before she could think about being left alone with Travis, he spoke again, his voice softer—and much closer than it should have been.

"Katie, I hope you know we weren't trying to embarrass you. It's just that we both enjoy your baking so much. No one else's baking comes close to being as delicious as yours."

Katie nodded her head furiously, answering in a small voice.

"I was not embarrassed by what you said—well, not entirely."

"Then something else has you upset?"

She shook her head again before answering, "What would make you think I am upset?"

"Because you're crying on your cookies." He spoke softly, his voice filled with concern.

He must have moved closer to Katie while he was speaking because she could feel a soft breath against her neck as he spoke.

She moved away from the cookies and began to search for a towel to dab at the cookies. After locating a towel and giving herself a *gut* internal pep talk, Katie turned back to face Travis—just as Freida walked back into the room, chattering as she came.

Thankful the awkward moment had passed, Katie nodded to herself and turned to carefully dab at the cookies that were rapidly cooling on the open rack in front of her.

"Can you believe how much there is left for us to do, Katie? We have the dresses to finish and you have the cake to bake and there are a dozen other things. I am for certain going to forget something."

Katie looked back at Freida and smiled. "For sure and for certain, you don't need to worry about that. Your *mamm* will not forget one thing."

Freida laughed before she responded. "You are right about that. She probably has lists of the lists she has made."

They all laughed at that, though an uncomfortable silence quickly replaced the laughter when Freida pushed through the kitchen door.

Travis waited for Katie to speak—about the wedding, or her family—anything. But Katie remained silent. It was several long minutes before Travis finally broke the silence.

"Well, I guess I had better get to these deliveries." His voice sounded odd, but Katie said nothing for fear that she would only make things more awkward between them.

Just as he was loading up the last of the deliveries, the phone rang. Katie listened for a moment—and when no one answered it, she went to pick up the kitchen extension.

She was surprised to hear Mr. O'Neal's nephew on the other end.

"Has Travis gone out yet with his deliveries?"

Katie was surprised by the question to be sure; immediately she was reminded of all the times Mr. O'Neal had *kumme* in to the bakery, asking about where Mrs. Simpkins had gone. . . how he could reach her. . . when she would be back. . . and so many other questions, Katie could not possibly remember them all.

Wondering about it, she answered Sean's question—as she tried to think of a way she could find out what was going on. "Not yet. He is almost finished loading up now."

"Great. Could you ask him to deliver Uncle Andrew's order too, please."

"*Jah*, I can do that." His rushed tone had her worried now. "Is everything all right?" Katie worried that her being unable to answer Mr. O'Neal's questions had made him angry with them.

But angry enough to stop picking up her orders? If only Mrs. Simpkins had not made us promise not to tell him where she has gone.

"No, everything is not fine. I do not know how Uncle Andrew does all of this by himself, but I cannot do it all. If you could just have Travis deliver that order, it's one less thing I have to worry about."

"*Jah,* I will tell him."

"Thanks, Katie." And with that, he hung up—without even saying goodbye.

Katie shook her head as she moved to the back door and called to Travis.

TWO

Travis set down the box he was holding before turning back toward the bakery, surprised to hear Katie asking him to come back in.

When he opened the door, she was just walking out of the walk-in cooler with a large box Travis was certain he recognized.

"What is it, Katie?"

"Sean just called. He wants you to please deliver Mr. O'Neal's order."

"But Andrew always picks up his Friday order."

Katie was already nodding, "*Jah,* he does, but Sean asked if we would please deliver it."

"Did he say why?"

This time Katie was shaking her head before he finished. "He did not say, but he sounded a bit odd."

Travis shook his head in return, but took the box from Katie. "What could be going on?"

Katie opened her mouth, but closed it before she said anything, giving a slight shake of her head as she did.

"Is there something you are not telling me Katie-girl?"

When she only shook her head again, Travis pressed. "Katie?"

"*Ach.* All right. I am worrying about whether or not Mr. O'Neal is angry with us. He has been in the bakery nearly every day since Mrs. Simpkins left, trying to get us to tell him where she went."

When she said nothing else, Travis asked, "And?"

"Well, we promised Mrs. Simpkins that we would not tell him where she has gone—so we have not."

"Is there more to that?" The confusion was beginning to make him dizzy.

"*Jah*, there is more to it. I am afraid we may have made Mr. O'Neal angry when we would not tell him how he can reach Mrs. Simpkins."

"So, you think he is angry at you; that is why he wants me to deliver his order?"

"*Jah*." Katie nodded again.

"But wouldn't he just cancel his order if he were angry at you?"

"I thought perhaps he would still need the order for his High Tea today. But mayhaps he will be canceling his next order."

"Ah, I see the problem." Travis smothered a laugh at how confusing the whole thing was.

He did not see any reason to think that

Mr. O'Neal, who was a business man, would be angry over something so simple, but he was not going to argue with Katie.

He leaned towards her to whisper, "Would you like me to try and find out what is going on when I deliver his order?"

Katie smiled then for the first time today. "*Jah*, would you? That would be just *wunderbaar*. Oh, and can you throw these away? For sure and for certain, I cannot serve them to customers now."

She moved to the counter and dumped the tear-stained cookies in a paper bag, before turning back and handing them to Travis.

He laughed. "Not for anything in the world would I be throwing away some of your cookies!"

"But you must. They are ruined."

"Go on about your work, Katie-girl. Don't give these cookies another thought. I'll get rid of them for you. Go bake another batch."

He turned then, smothering a smile—and

heard Katie push through the kitchen doors, calling out Freida's name as she went.

When Travis arrived at the back door of the cafe, he could see right away that things were not quite right.

The door was open. Andrew O'Neal never left the back door of the cafe open. Someone inside was speaking, loudly... roughly... almost yelling. And they were not speaking English.

He knocked on the door and waited, looking at his watch as he did so. It was less than a minute before Sean appeared at the door, still speaking the strange language, which must have been his native tongue, which Travis understood exactly nothing.

"Thank you, Travis. You've no idea how much I appreciate this. Could you just set it there, please." He motioned to the only empty space in the kitchen, which looked as if a tornado had swept through it.

"Is everything all right, Sean?"

"All right? No, everything is not all right. Uncle Andrew has been gone for two days now, and I am certain it has something to do with the argument we had on Tuesday."

Sean ran a hand through his hair before going on. "It was a big misunderstanding, but he rushed out of here and left in a hurry. I finally got him on his cell, but he hung up before I got any answers and I've not heard from him since."

He stopped, took a breath and then went on. "I don't know, man. I'm not sure I can do this." He swept a hand around the room—and Travis could see how the young man was struggling to hold on to his composure.

"Doesn't Mr. O'Neal have some other help? A cook or a waiter or someone?"

"Aye, that he does, but he called in sick today." He lowered his voice a bit before adding, "Between you and me, I think he might just be thinking of looking for another job. And without knowing where Uncle Andrew is. . . or when he will be back. . . I don't exactly have any way to change his mind or anything.”

Travis had no idea what to say about any of it. It was all too shocking. Mr. O'Neal might be a bit of a mystery, but he had never struck Travis as being irresponsible.

There has to be some sort of explanation.

“What can I do to help? Anything?”

“This order is a big help. I managed to get through lunch, but it was no easy thing. What I am most concerned over is this High Tea. I know how seriously ladies take this thing. I don't want to mess it up.” He ran a hand through his hair again as he looked at Travis with a look of such misery, which made him all the more determined to help however he could.

“Well, I do know that there are usually only three or four ladies who come to the tea on Friday. Most of what is in that box is for tomorrow. That will be the tough one.”

"Aye, I know the Saturday High Tea is a big deal around here."

"So, for today you just need a bit of help serving, then?"

"Aye, I already have everything ready for the tea. I'll clean up all this mess later."

They both looked at the disaster in the kitchen. Travis could not help but think of how Katie would panic at such a sight. She would never have allowed a kitchen to become such a mess—and she certainly would not leave it this way for long.

She would just roll up her sleeves and start cleaning.

He thought about the one order he still had to deliver. He had planned to go by the bakery afterwards, but he immediately changed his plans.

"Listen, Sean, I have one more delivery I have to make, but that's it for the day. And I don't have any other odd jobs lined up for the afternoon. How about if I come back and help you?"

"That would be a miracle. And I would be forever in your debt."

"High Tea starts at three, right?"

"Aye, that it does. Three o'clock sharp. Will you be back by then?"

Travis was already nodding. "If I scoot right now, I can be back by then."

Sean walked with him to the door. "I really appreciate this, man. You'll never know how much."

Travis nodded again, but kept moving towards the delivery van. "I'll be back before you know it. In the meantime, work on that messy kitchen!"

———THREE———

Katie let her thoughts wonder a bit while she kneaded dough. The bell over the front door seemed to tinkle almost constantly, although they had only been open for about half an hour.

What is going on? It is much too early for the Saturday morning rush.

As she continued to work the dough, Katie wished Freida would let her in on what was happening. Since it was Saturday, Katie was especially busy and had very little time to do anything about it. She had dough to knead, cookies to bake, orders to get ready—and if the amount of customers so far this morning were any indication, they would likely be extra busy today.

It should have been a normal day, especially with nearly two weeks until the holiday.

Ha! It has been anything but business as usual since Mrs. Simpkins left for New York. I hope she is having a gut time, but I cannot wait for her to return.

There were times Katie almost regretted telling her dear, sweet boss that she and Freida could handle the bakery by themselves.

She had had no idea then, that Freida would be planning her wedding—for the day before Thanksgiving. And none of them could have anticipated the people from town coming in nearly every day, trying to find out where Mrs. Simpkins had gone and when she would return.

It was so rare for her to go on long trips —and even more unusual for her to essentially disappear with no one but Katie, Travis and Freida knowing where she had gone.

The first few days had been especially difficult, what with Mr. O'Neal coming in every day—especially since his visits had dwindled to almost none over the past few months.

Not that it is especially surprising, with how cold Mrs. Simpkins was to him whenever she saw him.

It still made no sense to Katie. No matter how she thought about the two of them, she could not figure out what had happened to mess up their budding romance.

One day, Mrs. Simpkins and Mr. O'Neal had been together. . . seemingly *froh*—happy. Freida had been talking as if they would be engaged any day. The entire town had pretty much been expecting an announcement any time from them.

And then—with absolutely no warning—they were fighting and sniping at each other, out in front of the bakery, or on one of the streets by the cafe. Whenever they came within ten feet of each other they would spend the whole time fighting—with absolutely no clue as to why.

And then Mrs. Simpkins had suddenly announced that she needed a vacation, asking Katie and Freida if they could handle the bakery alone for a few weeks.

Not that either of us would have told her nee. . .

That had been months ago. And since then, Mr. O'Neal's visits to the bakery had slowed considerably, until he only came in on days when Mrs. Simpkins was not there.

Then, last week, once he had figured out she was gone, he had come in every day trying to get either of them to tell him where she was and when she would be back.

Until Wednesday.

And then on Friday, his nephew had

called . . . *not Mr. O'Neal. . . but Sean. . .* to have his standing order delivered.

I hope Travis found out something about what has happened with Mr. O'Neal. . . and that he's not angry with me.

Katie kept working. . . and thinking. The bell in the front room kept tinkling and Freida kept popping in to snag muffins and bread that Katie had ready for her.

But Travis didn't show.

Katie had just about decided that she would need to call their backup driver—when Travis came in the back door.

"I am so sorry I'm late, Katie. I overslept."

She opened her mouth to ask him why, but he was already hurrying into the walk-in cooler, then rushing back out with his arms loaded down with white bakery boxes. A moment later, he disappeared out the back door.

Freida walked into the kitchen a second after the back door closed.

"Did I hear Travis? Is he finally here?"

Katie could only nod when the door opened again and Travis nearly ran past them both with barely a nod of acknowledgment.

"He overslept." Katie raised her hands in a motion of confusion at Freida's questioning look after he disappeared into the cooler again.

Less than a minute later, he rushed by them again, not looking at either girl as he pushed his way out the back door with more boxes.

"Katie, do you think we were right? Did he find out that Mr. O'Neal is angry with us and he does not know how to tell us?"

Katie started to tell Freida it could not be that, but she stopped herself before saying a word.

Could she be right? This is certainly not

normal behavior for Travis. And that call yesterday was certainly out of the ordinary for Mr. O'Neal.

"I don't know, Freida." She started to say more, but the door opened and Travis rushed by them again.

Freida turned and quickly followed him. She appeared a few seconds later with him in tow.

"Travis, enough of this. Tell us what is going on!" Freida only let him go once they stood next to Katie.

Katie watched as Travis looked from her. . . to Freida. . . and back to her again. After a moment, he threw up his hands in surrender.

"All right. I'll tell you what I know, but it's not much."

Neither girl said anything and after a few tense seconds, he went on.

"When I got to the cafe yesterday, Sean was there by himself. Mr. O'Neal was not there and Sean was frantic. Evidently his uncle left sometime Tuesday with no word to anyone and no one knows where he has gone."

"Is that all?" Katie pressed, hoping for more details that might tell them if it was their fault—or if it could be anything else.

"He and Sean had an argument. He stormed out of the cafe after lunch and did not come back. When Sean tried to call him, he answered, but rushed Sean off the phone and said nothing about where he was or when he would be back."

"You said Tuesday, *jah?*" Freida asked, her voice very quiet.

Katie thought back to Tuesday, the last day they had seen Mr. O'Neal. He had *kumme* into the bakery, asking again about where Mrs. Simpkins had gone. As promised, they had only said that they could not tell him. He had left abruptly and they had not seen him since.

"Yeah. Apparently he had come over here asking about where Mrs. Simpkins went.

Sean said he was in a foul mood when he walked back into the cafe—and they got into an argument. His uncle stormed out after that and no one has heard from him since."

"Katie, could he be angry with us?"

"I am afraid he might be, Freida."

Travis spoke up then. "Or it might not be. He did argue with Sean. Maybe something happened there that made him angry enough to leave."

Katie looked at Freida—who was looking right back at her. If she was reading her *freind's* expression right, she did not think that was likely either.

"Katie. . . Freida. . . stop. Don't jump to conclusions. We don't know what he was thinking. He could have just decided to take a trip—like Mrs. Simpkins did. Maybe all this fighting between them got to be too much for him too, and he just needed a break."

Freida was nodding slowly, but her expression did not look like she was totally convinced. . . which was exactly how Katie felt.

"Anyway, I overslept because I was helping Sean clean up the kitchen over at the cafe. It was a disaster."

"Well, that was very *gut* of you, Travis." Katie turned to face him then.

He waved away her praise. "It was no big deal."

"I am certain it was a very big deal to Sean. Without your help, it would have taken him at least two times as long."

"Yeah, about that." Travis looked away from Katie, and something in his behavior had her worried again.

"What is it Travis?"

"Well, it's like this. With Mr. O'Neal gone and Sean not really knowing what to do and me having some free time right now with no extra odd jobs to do, I told him I'd help him out at the cafe."

"But what about the deliveries?" Freida, panic filling her voice, spoke up before Katie could say a word.

"I can still do the deliveries in the morning. And I can do the afternoon deliveries too. I just might be a bit late getting started."

Freida still looked as if she was ready to panic, so Katie quickly spoke up. "That will work out just fine, I think. The afternoon deliveries can stand to be a bit late."

"Katie, are you sure?"

"*Jah,* Freida. There is nothing so urgent that it cannot wait an hour."

Travis let out a breath of relief and Katie turned back to him.

"So, you will do the morning deliveries here, and then go over to help Sean with lunch, *jah?*"

Travis nodded, but before he could speak, Katie went on.

"What about the High Tea today? Will you have time to do deliveries before—or will it have to wait until after?"

"That late in the afternoon might be too late for some people." Freida interrupted

Travis before he could answer.

Katie turned to her *freind,* trying to calm her concerns, but also confused about why she was so concerned about the deliveries.

"Freida, I think we can find some way to make it work. Travis, we only have two deliveries scheduled for this afternoon right now."

Freida started to speak up again, but Katie interrupted her this time. "Even if we receive more, we can find a way to make it work."

Travis spoke then. "I was just going to say that I could always take care of any deliveries we have between lunch and the High Tea."

"That sounds like the perfect solution. Mr. O'Neal always says that lunch is winding down by half past one."

"Exactly. That should be plenty of time for me to take care of any deliveries that cannot wait."

After a moment, Katie added, "And if

there are no deliveries that need immediate delivery, you could just stay at the cafe—and take care of things after the High Tea.”

Travis was nodding, but Freida still looked more than a little apprehensive about the situation. Shrugging her shoulders, she turned and headed back to the front room without saying anything.

“Is she going to be all right? She seemed pretty upset.” Travis looked concerned.

“*Jah*, for sure she will be *allrecht*.” Katie assured him. “I will talk with her.”

FOUR

Freida barely spoke to Katie after Travis left to make the morning deliveries. She breezed through the doors to the kitchen occasionally to pick up cookies and bread that was ready for the display case out front —or to retrieve a special order, but she never stayed long.

Since Travis had left the bakery, Katie's thoughts had strayed to him—and their odd situation—more than a few times. The news he had given them about Mr. O'Neal was not at all reassuring.

He was gone, and no one knew when he would return. . . or even if he would. It was not a comforting thought.

Even less comforting was Freida's reaction to Travis' news this morning. She had been far more concerned than Katie would have expected from someone who should have been thinking about her upcoming wedding.

Perhaps she is just upset over the misunderstanding with Mr. O'Neal.

That would make sense. Without knowing the reason behind Mr. O'Neal's sudden disappearance, it was all too easy to imagine the worst.

Even though she was trying not to be, she was concerned too.

She was also worried over what Mrs. Simpkins would think of losing Freida's help for several months and what she would say about losing Travis to the cafe. . . even if only for the afternoons.

She will never leave me in charge again.

Still, Katie had to wonder why Freida was so panicked over the deliveries. There were plenty of days they did not see Travis all afternoon because he had other odd jobs to attend to. He was almost always available for the morning deliveries, but he had even missed a few mornings over the past year, since he had started helping out.

Perhaps Freida is worried because Mr. O'Neal is missing and Mrs. Simpkins is not here and she knows we will be busy for Thanksgiving.

At least. . . that was the only reasoning that made sense to her.

Or perhaps she is feeling the stress of not being ready for the wedding.

"Katie, is the order ready for the mayor's wife?"

Freida's voice shook Katie out of her thoughts and had her turning towards the cooler. She took several steps before she remembered that her hands were covered in flour and little bits of dough.

"I will take that as a yes." Freida smothered a laugh and Katie could only nod as she turned back to the tall prep table and the dough she had been working.

As Katie went back to her dough, Freida pulled open the heavy cooler door and walked inside to retrieve the order. She emerged a few moments later, a large box in hand, and then she was pushing through the swinging doors. . . just as Travis opened the back door.

Katie turned towards him in surprise.

"Travis, for certain, lunch cannot be over with yet. Not on a Saturday."

Travis laughed as he turned, revealing a large basket he had concealed behind him. "Sean sent lunch as a thank you." He set the basket down on the empty prep table by the back door. "I have to get right back. I just took advantage of a break in business to drop that by. There's nothing in there that will spoil quickly so you just get to it when you can."

"*Danki*. Be sure to tell Sean we appreciate it."

"I will. And I'll see you later to get those deliveries." He was halfway out the door when Katie called to him.

"Travis, there are no deliveries that can't wait until after the High Tea. You're going to be so busy with lunch. Do not worry about running back over here in between."

"Are you sure, Katie?"

Katie was nodding before he finished. "For sure and for certain, Travis. They can wait until the High Tea is finished."

He stepped back in a bit and Katie added, "I am for certain, Travis. Go—before you are late."

"All right, then. I'll see you after tea time."

"*Jah,* that sounds *gut*. See you then."

With a last nod, he slipped out the door. It closed behind him just as Freida walked back into the kitchen.

"Katie, did I hear someone's voice?"

"*Jah,* you heard Travis. Sean sent us a lunch." She motioned to the basket he had left for them.

"Did he pick up any of the afternoon deliveries?"

"*Nee,* he had to rush right back."

Freida said nothing, just turned and walked back through the swinging doors.

It was late afternoon before Travis came back. Katie just happened to pull a tray of cookies out of the oven as the back door opened.

"Travis, it's *gut* to see you. How did High Tea go?"

"It was good. Busy. Did you enjoy the lunch Sean sent over?

"*Jah,* it was *wunderbaar gut.*"

"*Gut*—I mean good. Katie I hate to bother you, but have you seen my sister lately?"

The question—and the worry in Travis' voice—threw Katie completely off balance.

"I saw her a few days ago, when she came by the bakery looking for you. Since then. . . *nee*, I have not." Katie shrugged as she answered, surprised at the worry in her *freind's* voice.

"Not at all? Not even from a distance? Maybe somewhere in town?"

"*Nee*. I have not, Travis. Is everything all right with Gwen?"

"To tell you the truth, Katie, I don't know. She disappears all the time lately. I don't even know if she's going to school when she's supposed to or not."

He raked a hand through his already unruly hair before going on.

"I have no idea what's going on with her lately. She's never home when she should be. She comes in late every night. And all she does is make excuses. And that's when I can get her to talk to me, which isn't very often. Mostly she just slinks off to her room and ignores me.”

“I am sorry, Travis. I wish there was some way that I could help.”

“Thanks, Katie. That means so much to me. I wish I could think of some way you could help.”

At the squeak of the swinging door, both Katie and Travis turned when Freida walked into the kitchen.

“Freida, have you seen my sister lately?”

Katie cringed at the worry in Travis' voice. Knowing how excited and *froh* Freida had been for weeks now, Katie was not at all certain her *freind* would respond accordingly.

She was not wrong.

Freida nearly sang out when she answered. “*Nee*, Travis. I haven't seen her at all lately. Why?”

Travis didn't answer and Katie started to speak up, but she could see that Freida was hardly paying either of them any mind. She was clearly in a world of her own, thinking about the wedding. . . or Thomas. . . or both.

Katie slowly kneaded the dough in front of her, watching Travis carefully as he stacked boxes for more deliveries. His mouth was moving, but there was no sound that she could hear.

Perhaps he is talking to himself.

She only wished there was some way to help him—and Gwen.

Gwen is such a sweet maedel.

At the same time, she thought about the last singing she had attended, the one where Gwen had *kumme* with some of her *freinden*. They had all been dressed very inappropriately, no doubt trying to look much older than they were, but clearly with no idea that young Amish *buwes* did not pay any mind to such ridiculous clothing.

I hope she is not involved in anything dangerous.

"I just wish I knew where she was going all the time." Travis spoke quietly, under his breath, but Freida was close enough to hear and it pulled her out of her own thoughts.

"Have you even asked her, Travis?"

Katie shook her head at her *freind's* question. She wanted to laugh at the innocence in Freida's words, but given that there were no younger children in her family, Freida really had no way of knowing how pointless it was to question teenagers about their activities.

Living with several siblings—both younger and older *bruders* and *schweschders*, Katie knew first hand that teenagers were only cooperative when they felt like it—and no amount of questioning would change that.

Fortunately, Travis was either too distracted or he chose to ignore Freida's question.

"Travis, I don't think Gwen would do anything bad or dangerous."

When Travis said nothing, Katie went on. "I'm sure there must be a reasonable explanation for where she has been going. . . and for what she is doing."

Travis looked up at Katie, hope evident in his eyes. "Do you think so?"

Katie nodded immediately. "I do. I really do. Gwen is a *gut maedel*."

"She is. I know that." He spoke softly, almost under his breath again.

"I have deliveries." Travis spoke quickly and quietly as he turned away from the two of them and headed for the back door.

Katie watched him go, still wishing there was something she could do for him. For sure and for certain, she would be thinking of him—and praying for his family—tonight and tomorrow at the Sunday service.

FIVE

Travis followed the dusty road to the Yoder's farm. He had finished the Monday morning deliveries quicker than he had expected to—and now he needed to talk to a friend.

It was actually a bit surprising that Jake was the first name that came to mind when he thought of a friend nearby. But since moving from the city, he had completely lost touch with most of his friends there.

Not that I had all that many people who I

could talk to about something like this anyway.

Friends he had made in the city had either come from small families or they had been an only child. None of them would understand how it felt to be in his shoes; responsible for his brothers and sisters while his mother slowly regained her health.

At least Jake understood responsibility.

That is one thing these plain folks teach their kids early. Wish I could figure out their secret.

He slowed the car as he drove along the gravel drive that he had driven many times over the past couple of months, thinking about how he had met Jake. At the time, he had no idea that Jake was Amish.

Nothing about that first meeting had given Travis the first clue that his new friend lived on a farm, raised chickens, helped grow his own food and dressed like someone from colonial times.

Only after moving back home, had Travis

discovered the truth to his new friend's upbringing. To say it had been an eye-opener was a huge exaggeration.

However, it had not taken long for the two of them to discover that the differences in their childhood had very little bearing on their friendship.

Before he reached the end of the drive, two boys he recognized as Jake's brothers were racing out to the car, waving wildly.

Probably wondering if I brought any treats from the bakery with me.

He stopped the car by the new chicken house he had helped Jake finish earlier in the year. He was still amazed at the size of the structure that held nothing but chickens.

The two boys—whose names he could never seem to remember—leaned in the car window, excitedly throwing out questions, talking over each other until he held up a hand in surrender.

Thankfully, before the boys could launch into any more questions, Jake came around the side of the barn and raised a hand in greeting.

He said something to the two boys in their native language—which Travis still only understood a handful of words—and they went running off toward the fields.

"Hey, Travis. You *kumme* out to help with the chickens?"

He said it with a laugh, one that Travis knew was at his expense. When Jake's uncle had delivered the chickens, Travis had offered to help transfer them from the truck.

He had had no idea what he was getting himself into—and the ruckus that followed had been almost more than he could handle.

Jake had not been the only Yoder laughing at Travis that day, either.

"Very funny, Jake. You're the one who didn't warn me."

"You *Englischers* are too easy sometimes."

Travis smiled. . . then joined in, laughing at how desperate he had felt that day.

Thankfully, Jake's family had understood. Jake and his brothers had handled most of the transfer.

When they stopped laughing, Travis remembered that he had come here to talk to Jake, to get his advice.

"Listen, can we talk about siblings a bit? I need some advice."

"Sure man. *Kumme* on back to the barn. I've got a couple of things I need to finish, but you can talk while I work."

Travis climbed out of the low vehicle and followed.

"I might even give you a hand."

When Jake laughed, Travis added, "As long as it doesn't involve chickens."

They laughed all the way to the barn.

Freida walked into the coffee shop across the street, waving to Hannah Kaufman—who was finishing up a customer's order—as she walked up to the long counter.

There was only one other customer in the shop, which Freida was thankful for. She did not like to leave work early, but she had begun to feel like she just had to get out of there.

Business had been especially brisk, and evenings and weekends she stayed busy trying to get everything ready for the wedding—and moving from her haus to the one she would be sharing with Thomas.

I need a break. I can't keep working sunup to sundown. Especially with no other help at the bakery. Katie would help, but she's so busy she can't leave the kitchen to help me out front.

"Hello, Freida. How is business going at the bakery?"

"Business is *gut,* Hannah—very *gut.* We are already busier than usual this week."

"You want your usual?"

Freida nodded and Hannah turned to begin pouring her *kaffe.*

"When does Mrs. Simpkins return?"

"Not for another week at least. I hope Katie and I can keep up with everything until she returns."

"Are you going to postpone your honeymoon trip until after she returns?"

"*Jah*. I don't see that there is anything else to do. For sure and for certain, Katie cannot do it all by herself. It's almost too much for the both of us. Honestly, I don't see how Katie and Mrs. Simpkins will be able to manage when I'm gone."

"Why doesn't she hire someone part-time to help out, especially during the busiest times? She will need someone when you leave anyway, won't she, or are you planning to continue working?"

"You know Hannah, that is a *wunderbaar* idea. Katie will need some help when I am gone. Even with Mrs. Simpkins back, the bakery will be too busy for just the two of them. I will talk to Katie about it. I am certain Mrs. Simpkins would approve."

"*Jah,* I am certain she would. And if you can get her trained in time, perhaps you would not have to put off your honeymoon trip."

"Thomas would like the sound of that."

"I am certain he would."

Both girls burst into laughter. Hannah handed Freida her *kaffe,* then pulled out a raspberry turnover, which she knew was Freida's favorite dessert.

"Here you go, Freida—enjoy your treat."

"Danki, Hannah. I will. Then I must get home. I have lots to do there."

Travis pulled the bandana from his back pocket and swiped at the sweat on his brow. Jake had taken him up on his offer of help, and though he had not planned on the work being quite so hard, he had to admit that it was helping him to work out his frustrations over his little sister.

A tightly-bound bale of hay landed on the floor next to Travis and he let out a short laugh at Jake's timing.

"Hey Jake, how many more of these?"

"That's the last one."

Travis laughed at the relief in his friend's voice. "I would have thought you'd be used to this kind of workload."

"You never really get used to it. You do it because it has to be done." Jake answered as he slid down the ladder to land beside Travis.

"Is that why you were in the city?" Travis turned so he could see Jake's face when he answered.

"Honestly. . ."

He didn't answer out loud, just nodded his head as Jake took one end of the hay bale and he hefted the other side.

"This is part of the reason, *jah*." His breath huffed out as the two of them dropped the bale of hay.

"So, you weren't sure you wanted to be a

farmer?"

"I wasn't sure I had what it takes to be a farmer. It's not the same thing."

Travis weighed his next words carefully. "What made you decide to come back?"

"When I was out there on *rumschpringe,* I worked a lot of different jobs." He pulled a sharp knife from the back pocket of his work pants and went to work on the thick baling wire before going on.

"I wanted to be sure I was making the right choice."

"Sounds sensible to me."

"*Jah,* it was the right thing. Do you know what I learned from all of those jobs?"

Travis shook his head in answer.

"I learned that it doesn't matter what job you have. All of them are hard. But this one, this job I can do."

Travis found himself nodding along with his friend. He would not have thought of that, but he could see where it made sense.

"So, Travis, what is it you were wanting

to ask me about earlier?"

And Travis realized that he didn't need to ask anymore. He knew what he needed to do.

──────── SIX ────────

The next morning, Katie looked up when the kitchen door swung open and Freida nearly danced through it.

She is certainly in a better mood than she was when she left yesterday. Maybe the extra rest helped.

"Katie," She practically sang the word.

"*Jah,* Freida?"

"I know what we need to do now. I was talking with Hannah before going home yesterday, and I think she has given us the solution to all of our troubles."

Intrigued, Katie looked at her *freind* and waited for her to go on.

"We need to hire more help for the bakery."

The sound of the bell over the front door of the bakery stopped Katie from responding, and Freida dashed out with a quick "*ach*" to help whoever had just *kumme* in.

While she was gone, Katie thought over the idea. It really wasn't so terrible. It would mean that Freida and Thomas could go on their honeymoon trip immediately—if they could find someone and get them trained in time.

And it's something we would have to do at some point, anyway. Even once Mrs. Simpkins is back, there is too much for her to keep up with in the office, for her to put in the kind of time that Freida does behind that counter, waiting on customers.

And for those who choose to stay; Freida

brings them refills of kaffe, chats with them a bit, then wipes off the table when they leave— all the while watching out for new customers.

And it isn't as if I can do the baking and wait on the customers, too. Lately it's been so busy, I never seem to have time to leave the kitchen.

She continued to ponder on the idea while she scooped cookie dough onto a lined cookie sheet.

I wonder who we could get. It would need to be someone who is gut with people, someone who knows their way around a cash register, and someone who knows the people in town well enough.

"Right, where was I?" Freida spoke as she moved through the doors, back into the kitchen.

"We need to hire some help. Who do you think it should be?"

"Well, I think the obvious choice would be Travis' young sister, Gwen. Travis would not worry so much over where she is if she is here. And we know she is a quick learner and *gut* with people. I think she would do a *wunderbaar* job."

Katie was shaking her head before Freida had even finished. "Freida, Gwen might seem like the obvious choice, but she is still in school.

"*Ach,* Katie, you are right. I did not even think of that."

"We could still ask her to help out. She could work in the afternoons and on Saturdays—and it would be a *gut* thing if Travis does not have to worry about her so much. If she is here, she is not out, getting into trouble."

"*Jah,* Katie, that is a *wunderbaar gut* idea."

"*Gut.* Now the next question is, who else can we get? We need to find someone who can work full-time to help out, too."

"I do not know of anyone who is needing a job now. Perhaps *Gott* will send us someone."

"*Jah,* that is just what I will pray for, Freida. And in the meantime, we should mention the idea to Travis. He will need to let Gwen know—and perhaps he knows of someone else who is in need of a job."

When Travis came in to pick up the afternoon deliveries, both girls were waiting to talk to him. The moment he stepped through the back door, the kitchen door swung open and Freida rushed through it.

"Hey Travis. We have something to talk to you about. Something I think you're going to like."

"I have lots of deliveries this afternoon, plus going by to help Sean at the cafe. Can it wait until later?"

"*Nee,* but we won't keep you too long." Katie assured him.

As quickly as they could, Katie and Freida shared their plans with Travis, including the hiring of a full-time counter person.

"Can you recommend anyone? Do you know of someone who has any experience, or is looking for work?" Katie asked.

"No, I can't think of anyone. But I can be on the lookout for someone." Travis replied. "And I can't wait to get home and tell Gwen the good news."

Heading towards the walk-in cooler, he stopped, then surprised both of the girls by rushing back over and giving them big hugs.

"Thank you, both of you, for thinking of Gwen. She's going to be so excited! And I can stop worrying so much about her."

Turning towards the cooler again, he quickly made his way inside. Almost immediately, he came out with his arms full of bakery boxes. After putting them in the delivery van, he came back to get two more loads of orders.

As the girls heard the van pull away, Freida started towards the double doors.

"Katie, I have another idea. Why don't we

make a sign and hang it in the window about looking for full-time help?"

"That's a *gut* idea, Freida. Do yo want to work on the sign when you don't have customers?"

"*Nee*, I think you should make it. Your lettering is much better than mine. And your artistic ability will make it look much nicer than anything I could do. I still remember how *wunderbaar gut* the display window looked when you painted it for Christmas."

"I think you could do a *gut* job on the sign. After all, it doesn't need to look fancy or anything."

"*Nee*, you do it."

"*Allrecht*, I'll do it. I'll work on it tonight at home and bring it in tomorrow."

Hearing the sound of a bell, Freida hurried back to the front room to wait on another customer.

Travis called out as he walked into the brightly lit house. As usual, Bobby was the first to reach him.

Travis braced himself for the boy-sized bullet, but Bobby did not plow into his big brother's legs like he had so many other times. He stopped in plenty of time, but he did throw his arms around Travis and hug him tightly so he didn't worry overmuch about the change in behavior.

"Is everybody home?"

"You mean Gwen, right?"

Travis was more than a little surprised at his baby brother's insightfulness, but he probably shouldn't have been. Bobby had heard the fights for himself, the hard words, the slamming doors.

And he's not exactly a little kid anymore. The sadness that overtook him at that thought was also a surprise. Why should he be sad that his little brother was growing up? Wasn't that what was suppose to happen?

Unless he goes through the same kind of stuff that Gwen is doing now.

That thought reminded him that he had two other brothers who would be going through puberty soon too—and they were already into so much trouble, Travis found he didn't even want to think of how that would change once they discovered the joys of spending time with girls.

For the moment, he held on tightly to his baby brother and tried to enjoy the simple hug.

"Yes, I mean Gwen. Is she here?"

"Yeah, she's in her room."

The undertone in Bobby's voice told Travis that she probably wasn't in the best of moods. He braced himself to deal with a surly teenager as Bobby ran off to play.

Moving through the house, Travis set down the basket of goodies Katie had sent with him in the kitchen.

After another deep breath, he turned down the hall and knocked on his sister's door. He heard the sound of muffled talking behind the door, and then what sounded like someone scrambling around the room.

He nearly knocked again, wondering what on earth his sister was up to, when the door opened and Gwen stood there looking up at him, breathless and flushed.

"I heard voices. Is there someone in there with you?"

"No. I was on the phone." Gwen waved their cordless extension as she answered.

Travis was tempted to press her, but decided that it would be better. . . easier. . . and probably smarter to just let it go.

"So, what did you need, Travis?"

He cleared his throat before answering. He didn't want to make it too easy on her.

"You know how Freida down at the bakery is getting married soon?"

"Yes. She invited me. Isn't that sweet of her?"

Gwen's smile was wider than he'd seen it in a while and Travis made a mental note;

first to thank Freida, and second to ask Katie why such a thing would make his baby sister so excited.

"And speaking of that, after the wedding, Freida and her new husband will be leaving on a honeymoon trip."

"I know. It sounds terribly romantic. I can't wait for my own honeymoon. It feels so far away." Her voice trailed off a little at the end. Travis used the opportunity to dive into what he really wanted to talk to her about.

"Right. Well, anyway, while Freida is away on her honeymoon, Katie needs some help down at the bakery."

That got her attention. She turned to him with eyes as big as he had ever seen them.

"Does she want me to be that help or does she want me to find her someone?"

"She wants you to be the help; well, at least part of the help."

"Oh Travis! Do you mean it? Really?"

"I mean it. They asked me this afternoon to talk to you about it."

"When do they want me to start?"

"Tomorrow."

"Really, that soon?"

"Yes, that soon. Katie needs time to train you before Freida leaves so she wants you to start as soon as possible."

Gwen threw herself at Travis, hugging him fiercely. "Just tell me when and I'll be there."

"Katie said right after school would be best."

He didn't tell her that Katie had only said that because she had been agreeing with him. Initially, she had said an hour after school let out would be early enough, but Travis liked the idea better of Gwen going straight to the bakery from school.

"That sounds great. I'll do that."

She turned away and started going through the piles of clothes that were strewn across almost every surface in her room.

"Oh, wow! I can hardly wait."

Travis watched for another minute before

deciding that he would never understand why everything about women. . . and girls. . . was so complicated and impossible to understand.

Shaking his head a little, he turned and went down the hall to the large family room where everyone else would be.

—————SEVEN—————

Katie arrived a little earlier than usual at the bakery on Wednesday. After placing the sign asking for help in the front window of the bakery, she watched for Travis to arrive while she mixed up dough for the day's bread loaves. He had been very certain his *schweschder* would say yes to the job, but Katie would not count those chickens before she had a firm answer from him.

While she worked she also thought about

her other worries. On the one hand, she was excited about working with Gwen. She was an exceptional young woman. She was polite and intelligent. She would be a *gut* addition to the bakery staff, even on a temporary basis.

On the other hand, if her *bruder's* suspicions were correct and she was getting into trouble, Katie worried that her working at the bakery could be a very bad idea.

Katie needed someone she could depend on in Freida's absence; someone who would *kumme* in to work on time, someone who could keep their mind on the job at hand, someone who could keep orders straight and keep customers *froh;* someone who would be an asset to them all.

Who could that person be?

Gott will send us the person we need.

She was pulled from her thoughts by the sound of the bell over the front door as Freida came in. The sweet sound of her *freind* singing put a smile on Katie's face—

despite her worries over Gwen . . . and Gwen's *bruder*.

"Is our new employee here yet?" Freida nearly sung out the words and Katie shook her head in answer.

"She will be in school this morning, Freida. Travis said he would make certain she came to the bakery straight after school."

Freida made a little *"hmm"* sound in the back of her throat before speaking. "Well, I don't know about you, but I am excited about it."

Katie decided that now would be a better time to voice her concerns to Freida—before Travis arrived for the day. "Aren't you the least bit worried about what Travis said?"

"What, that his *schweschder* has been getting into trouble lately and does not want to talk to him about what she is doing with her time?"

When Katie nodded, Freida went on. "*Nee*, I am not worried. She is a teenager. You have *bruders* and *schweschders*. How often do they tell your *mamm* and *dat* everything they are doing when they are not at home, especially during their *rumschpringe*?"

It was odd for Katie to think of her own *bruders* and *schweschders getting* into trouble, but she had to admit that Freida had a point.

"So, you think it will be all right?"

"*Jah*, I do. I think she will do a *gut* job. And who knows. . ." She shrugged and then went on. "Perhaps this will help with the rest of it too. Giving her responsibility can only be a *gut* thing, *jah*?"

"*Jah*." That was certainly true. Responsibility usually helped teenagers to grow up and act more responsibly.

"I hope Mrs. Simpkins is all right with this."

"She trusts you, Katie. She will be fine with it. How could she not be? You will need extra help. Even if you hire someone else to help you when I am away, they will not know the job as I do. Having Gwen to help too could only be a *gut* thing, *jah*?"

"I hope you are right."

"I am. Do not worry so much, Katie."

Freida went out to start setting up the front area and Katie kept working with the dough, still more than a little concerned that she was making a mistake.

Before she could worry about it too much however, the back door opened and Travis walked in with Gwen in tow.

"*Gut* morning Travis. . . Gwen. . ." Katie swallowed before speaking again. "I thought you would be in school this morning."

"Oh, yeah. Class starts at eight thirty. Travis said I could come in with him early today. I won't get in the way. I just want to watch. . . if that's okay."

Katie felt her worries begin to fade away. The young woman standing in front of her was more excited than Katie had ever seen her.

"Of course you can watch. I have only

just begun with the dough for the day so it might not be interesting for some time, but I will be glad of your company at least."

A moment later, she added, "Or, if you like, you could go out and watch Freida set up the front area."

"Why don't you do that, Gwen. Katie will have lots of batches of everything to make so you can always watch later."

Gwen nodded and pushed her way through the swinging doors. A moment later Gwen could be heard talking with Freida. Both voices were filled with excitement.

"Well, that is going to make Freida's day."

"Thank you, Katie."

"You—"

Travis interrupted Katie before she could finish, putting a hand over hers as he spoke. "No, Katie. Really. Thank you. You have no idea what this means to me."

He stopped, running a hand through his hair before going on. "I have been so worried about her—for awhile now. I think this is just what she needs right now."

"You sound as if I am saving her life, Travis."

"You never know, Katie. You just might be."

Katie shrugged off his comment, heat rushing into her cheeks at the very suggestion.

"I just want you to know that I appreciate what you are doing."

"I am happy to help out, Travis. It is the least I can do." A moment later, she added, "Not to mention, I really do need the help."

"Yeah, there is that." Travis sighed. "Well, I guess I need to get the morning deliveries loaded into the van and get our new employee on her way to school."

Freida looked up at the tinkle of bells

over the door, happy to see a new customer.

"Welcome to the Sweet Shop." She sang out, watching the young woman as she walked across the room quickly. "What can we help you with today?"

"Umm, a job?"

"You are looking for a job?"

The young woman looked at Freida a bit strangely before answering.

"Yes, the young woman over at the coffee shop said you were looking for someone to help out."

"*Jah,* we are. Do you live in town?"

"I just rented a room from Mrs. Mueller."

Freida nodded her head smartly, knowing Mrs. Mueller would not have rented a room to just anyone off the street. She would have checked the young woman out.

"I'll just go get Katie. Have yourself a seat." With that, she turned and pushed through the swinging doors.

"Katie, there is a young woman here about a job."

"A woman? Is it someone we do not know?"

"*Jah,* but she is renting a room from Mrs. Mueller. You know how she is about people she does not know. If she rented that young girl her room. . ." She shrugged and then went on. "I do not think we have anything to worry about."

"*Jah,* you are probably right, Freida."

"At least *kumme* and talk to her, Katie."

"All right, Freida, I will talk to her." She walked to the sink, flipping on the water and scrubbing the flour off her hands.

Less than a minute later, she was walking through the swinging doors and into the front area of the bakery.

— EIGHT —

Katie looked over the young woman who was perched right on the edge of her seat, her back to the front door of the bakery. She stood up so quickly when she saw Katie, she almost knocked the chair to the floor.

She turned to look at the chair and then turned back to Katie with a smile that was somewhere between apology and anxiety, holding out a hand in front of her.

Katie took it, more than a little surprised

at the feel of the young woman's hand. Her skin was soft to the touch, but her grip was surprisingly strong.

"Why don't we sit down?"

When they had both settled into their chairs, Katie took another look at the young woman. She was dressed neatly, but her clothes looked finely made, not at all what the typical teenager in their small town would wear.

Of course, she is a stranger to our town. Perhaps she is only trying to make a gut impression.

"Why don't we start with introductions. . . I am Katie Chupp. And you are?"

"My name is Bella Stanton."

Katie waited for her to go on, but she only sat there, looking at Katie expectantly.

"Bella, where are you from? What brings you to our town?"

She looked down before answering, and when she did speak, her voice was very quiet. "I was just looking for a change."

"Well, I can understand that.

"How old are you?"

"I am nineteen. I have graduated from high school. I meant to start college this fall, but it. . ." She stumbled over her words for several seconds before going on. "It just didn't work out."

She looked as if she wanted to take back some of what she had said, but obviously she could not so she sat there quietly, waiting for Katie to speak.

"Well, that happens. Sometimes we make plans, but *Gott* has other plans for us. If we follow His plans, things have a way of working out."

The young girl nodded, but didn't speak.

"Do you have any experience working in a bakery?"

"No, not really."

Before Katie could say anything, she added, "But I have had several summer jobs where I worked with the public so I could probably take care of customers with very little training. I wouldn't need to know how to bake for that, right?"

Katie nodded, oddly impressed that the young woman would get so excited about just the possibility of getting the job.

Let's hope she is as enthusiastic when she discovers the job could very well be temporary.

It was almost with reluctance that Katie asked a question she was hoping would shed the greatest light on whether or not it was a *gut* idea to hire the young woman.

"Freida tells me that you're renting a room from Mrs. Mueller?"

Bella's face lit up, which took Katie completely by surprise. Mrs. Mueller had her *gut qualities*—or at least Katie hoped so—but rarely did any of the people in the community light up when asked about the town busybody.

"Oh, yes. She is just the most wonderful lady. She and I talked for a long time. She said I was just the sort of person she had been looking for to rent out her spare room.”

Something about the way she said the words, coupled with the brilliant smile on her face, told Katie she was being completely honest, and not just telling Katie what she wanted to hear. And somehow Katie knew it was a sign of sorts.

Throwing caution to the wind, she decided to trust that this was *Gott's* way of telling Katie to take the chance.

“I should tell you that Mrs. Simpkins, the Sweet Shop's owner, is away on vacation right now so I cannot guarantee that she will make the job permanent.”

When Bella said nothing, just nodded enthusiastically, Katie went on.

“All right then, at least until Mrs. Simpkins returns, we would love to have your help.”

Bella jumped out of her seat again, sending the chair wobbling in place as she pumped Katie's hand.

"Oh, thank you, Miss Chupp."

The title surprised Katie, especially since the plain community only used those sorts of titles when dealing with *Englischers*.

"Just Katie, please."

"Okay, then. Katie, thank you. You have no idea how much this means to me. And I will work very hard. You'll see. I promise."

"I will hold you to that, I'm afraid. We will have a very busy week coming up, with the holiday and Freida's wedding and Mrs. Simpkins still away."

"When do you want me to start?"

"You could start right now if you want. The afternoon rush will begin soon, so I will ask Freida to show you the basics of how things go, how to work the cash register, that sort of thing—and then when the rush begins you can help as much as you are comfortable with."

The young woman nodded along with every word Katie said, looking a little more *naerfich* with each word.

"Unless you want to go change before getting started. . ."

Bella looked down at her clothes, then back up at Katie.

"Is this outfit not appropriate?"

Katie had to smother a laugh at the sincerity and confusion in the young woman's voice. "There is nothing wrong with your clothes. I should probably warn you now that working in a bakery can be messy."

"Oh! I didn't even think about that. I will go change. Most of my stuff is still in my car." She started backing toward the front door as she spoke. "I'll be right back." And with a quick turn, she was out the door.

When the bells over the door tinkled, Freida walked out of the kitchen.

"So, you decided not to hire her?"

Katie turned to Freida. "*Nee*, I decided *to* hire her. She went to change her clothes."

"What was wrong with her clothes?"

"They were a bit fancy, don't you think? Working here, even out front, can get messy."

"We have aprons." Freida laughed as she said it.

"*Gut* point. I did not think of that. And I'm used to working in the kitchen, where even an apron doesn't always keep my clothes from getting messy."

Looking back towards the front door, Katie asked, "Do you think she is telling the truth about just wanting a change of scenery? You don't think she could be running away from something, do you?"

Freida said nothing for what felt like a very long minute. When she spoke, she seemed to put a lot of thought into it.

"I think that Mrs. Mueller can get almost anything out of a person, no matter how hard they try to hide it—so if there is something to know, we will soon know it."

After a few seconds, she added, "You are not worried about hiring her, are you?"

Katie thought over her answer carefully before speaking. "I am more worried about

Bella. If she is running or hiding out, are we helping her by giving her a job or making matters worse. And if there's a problem, will we be able to help her when the time *kummes?*"

"Don't worry so, Katie. *Gott* will help us find a way."

"*Jah*, that is true."

No one was more surprised than Katie when the biggest uproar that day happened when Travis dropped Gwen off at the bakery.

He fairly stormed into the kitchen, the swinging doors banging against the wall on either side.

"Katie, just who is that out there with Freida?"

It took almost a minute for Katie to make her mouth work, so surprised she was by the unexpected behavior from Travis.

"She is Freida's replacement."

"I thought Gwen was supposed to be Freida's replacement."

Katie took a step back at the harsh tone in his voice. She had never heard him speak this way to anyone, even when his *bruders* had broken into the bakery and stolen all of the Independence Day cupcakes along with as much bread, cookies and other treats as they could carry.

"Travis, Gwen cannot be Freida's replacement. She is in school most of every day. Bella. . ."

He interrupted her, his voice still much too hard, but a bit less harsh, "Bella. . . really? What kind of name is that?"

"It is her name. Really, Travis. What is the problem? We still want Gwen to help out —especially with the holiday rush next week. Bella is just an extra help so that Freida can go on her honeymoon trip on time and Mrs. Simpkins will not *kumme* back to a disaster."

He started to speak, but when Katie tilted her head and put a flour-covered hand on her hip in defense, he stopped and stepped back a bit.

"It took me by surprise, that's all."

Katie swallowed the laugh that leapt to her lips. He looked like a young *buwe* pouting because he had just found out he had to share his new toy.

"It will work out just fine, Travis. Trust me."

"I do trust you, Katie-girl. I was just not expecting this today."

Katie nodded and Travis turned to head over to the walk-in cooler. Katie turned back to her bread, a wide smile taking over her face.

———————NINE———————

Monday morning, bright and early, Katie turned the corner in front of the Coffee Cup. She came to an abrupt stop when she saw that both Gwen and Bella were waiting for her at the front door of the bakery.

On the one hand, she was excited to see that they were both so eager. On the other hand, she was a bit worried that they were in some sort of competition.

Travis' words came back to her; about

the surprise and hurt he had felt over her hiring someone else to work with them. Was it possible he was responsible for Gwen showing up early? Could he have misunderstood what she had said the other day? Was he worried she would decide they didn't need Gwen's help anymore?

Why does he not trust me?

Putting a smile on her face, she continued on to the bakery, pulling the keys out of her apron pocket as she went.

Both girls jumped up from the steps at her approach.

"Good morning, Katie." they chorused together.

Katie stifled a laugh, but breathed a little easier at the smiles on both faces in front of her.

They looked like the best of *freinden*.

Perhaps they have been sitting here getting to know each other while they waited for me.

That could be a very gut thing. If they

become freinden, Travis will know he has nothing to worry over about Gwen's job.

"You know, neither of you have to be here this early."

"We know." They spoke at the same time again, and then they laughed together.

"We just want to watch and learn." Bella told Katie. Gwen nodded in agreement.

"All right. *Kumme* on in, then." She unlocked the door and walked into the dark bakery, snapping on the lights after entering.

Bella and Gwen followed Katie, but stopped in the front room and started lifting down the chairs—righting them and sliding them gently under the tables, while Katie continued on to the kitchen.

Katie let out a breath of relief. She looked forward to her quiet mornings when Freida came in just before opening time. In as busy a household as her home was, quiet was a rarity.

While Katie started her morning routine, the sound of chair legs moving on the floor continued.

She pulled the clipboard off the wall with the list of late orders and scanned through it, making a mental note of what needed to be prepared first, along with the regular morning baking.

Just as she started lining up ingredients along the prep table, Gwen came through the swinging doors.

"Will it bother you if Bella and I watch you start the baking? We really do want to learn."

Katie nodded and resigned herself to having no quiet time for the morning. She just couldn't tell Gwen no. She didn't want to give the girls the wrong impression. And she felt that Travis might take it the wrong way, too.

"Thank you, Katie. We'll stay out of the way." And with that, Gwen pushed back through the swinging doors, returning less than a minute later with Bella right behind her.

At eight o'clock sharp, Travis opened the back door to the bakery kitchen and walked in, fully prepared to get an ear-full from Katie for dropping off his sister so early.

She had been acting more than a little weird since he'd cornered her about the new girl she had hired without any warning.

Between his worry over making ends meet, his mother still being so frail, finding a way to keep his brothers out of trouble, and the new hours he was putting in to help Mr. O'Neal's nephew, he barely knew what he was doing from one minute to the next. He did not need to start worrying about Gwen having a job—or not having a job—because of some new girl in town.

Didn't Katie know he had enough to worry about already?

The first thing he noticed was a complete and total lack of. . . Katie. She was nowhere in the kitchen.

The second thing he noticed was the note taped to a stack of bakery boxes on the prep table closest to back door.

> *"Travis, I know what a hurry you're in this morning and since I had so much extra help, we stacked these up to make it easier for you. We have a few late deliveries today, but nothing urgent so don't feel like you have to rush back after lunch at the cafe."*
>
> *Katie.*

Dropping the note on the hard, metal surface, Travis turned and walked out of the kitchen, slowing only when he saw that there were customers in the bakery.

He watched for several minutes as Freida took orders and the new girl rushed off to put the order together. He had to admit, she was quick, quiet and kept a sweet smile on her face the entire time. . . albeit a nervous one.

When Freida noticed him standing there, she walked over to him, a wide smile on her face.

"Isn't she great? Truly an answer to a prayer."

He wanted to argue, but couldn't bring himself to mess up the happiness evident on Freida's face so he nodded.

"We stacked up the deliveries for you. Did you find everything all right?"

He nodded again and Freida went on, sounding more and more excited as she talked.

"Bella and Gwen are both such *wunderbaar gut* help. We got the bakery ready to open in record time so we figured we would make things a bit easier for you. We even opened up ten minutes early."

"That's great, Freida. Listen, where is Katie? Isn't she usually here this time of morning?"

"She is at the Coffee Cup, taking a break.

Bella and Gwen were such *gut* help, she took her break early this morning. She even walked Gwen to school, too, so you would not have to worry over her."

"Thanks Freida. I'll be back in a few minutes."

"All right, Travis." Freida smiled and went back over to the counter as the bell over the front door jingled and another customer walked in.

Travis went out through the front door, feeling silly the whole time. It was ridiculous to feel that he had to speak with Katie right this minute. There was nothing he really needed to say to her, but he felt the desire consuming him—and he was not about to ignore it.

He crossed the street and made his way to the Coffee Cup in the early morning light, watching the townspeople as he went. There was quite a crowd heading for the bakery this morning.

I know they're usually crowded, but this

is a bit much. Could all this really just be the holiday?

He didn't remember last Thanksgiving being this crowded.

What could it be?

A few minutes later, walking through the Coffee Cup, he figured out what it was. No one was talking loudly about it—and no one who was sitting too near Katie was talking about it at all, but there were definitely more than a few people in the coffee shop talking about the new girl over at the bakery.

Well, I guess that makes sense. She's new in town and the people are going to be curious until she's no longer a mystery.

Finally he made it over to where Katie sat, a coffee cup in one hand, one of her own muffins in the other.

"Hi, Katie."

She looked up, clearly surprised to see him there.

"Hi, Travis. Is everything all right?"

"Why wouldn't everything be all right?"

He pulled out a chair at her small table and scooted it around next to her, settling himself casually.

She looked at him with a slightly odd expression for several seconds before saying anything.

"I guess I just wondered why you're here, when you're usually out making deliveries by now."

"Well, you and your new helpers saved me quite a lot of time by stacking everything up by the back door, so I figured I could take a few minutes before I get going on that."

"Hmm." was her only response.

He sat there looking at her for almost a minute before he started to feel silly. When he realized he was just staring at her, and that she wasn't saying a word, he decided it was time to go.

"Well, I guess I'd better get to those deliveries then."

"*Jah.*" was all Katie said in return.

He stood, moved the chair back around to

it's original position and turned to go.

"I'll see you later, Travis."

"Yeah, later." And he made a hasty retreat, suddenly feeling very foolish.

The ball of dough Katie had been shaping hit the floor with a splat as she turned toward the front of the store at the sound of Freida's scream.

Only a moment later, Bella stuck her head in through the swinging doors. "Katie, you might want to come out here."

"Is everything all right?"

Bella didn't get a chance to answer because the next second Freida could be heard shouting "She's back! She's back!" so loudly Hannah probably heard her across the street at the Coffee Cup.

Katie waved a hand when Bella started to speak again. "I got it. Thank you."

She wiped her hands on the apron at her

waist as best she could, while rushing out of the kitchen.

The sight that greeted her was one of carefully organized pandemonium. Freida and Gwen were holding hands and jumping up and down in place, giggling and squealing right next to Mrs. Simpkins and Mr. O'Neal, who were, thankfully, laughing at the spectacle before them.

Bella stood behind the counter, both arms crossed in front of her as she watched all that was going on in front of her with what Katie hoped was amusement.

Katie rushed over to hug Mrs. Simpkins, laughing with her at the antics of Freida and Gwen, who were still jumping up and down and shouting.

It was several minutes before the scene quieted down enough for any meaningful conversation to be heard. Katie rushed to be heard first, afraid if she did not jump right in with her questions, she might never be able to.

"You're back early. Is everything all right? How was the cruise?"

She put a hand over her mouth, realizing what she had just said—and with Mr. O'Neal standing right there.

"It's quite all right, Katie. Andrew knows all about the cruise." And her boss shocked Katie by turning and smiled up at Mr. O'Neal, slipping her hand into his at the same time.

"I think we should tell them our news, Milly dear, before Katie begins to think you've taken leave of your senses."

And Katie could not believe her ears when her boss, Amelia Simpkins giggled.

Seeing their own Mrs. Simpkins holding Andrew's hand, Freida and Gwen stopped jumping up and down. "What news?" Freida asked, as they all crowded in close to Katie to hear the news.

Mr. O'Neal looked over at Mrs. Simpkins and Mrs. Simpkins looked back at him. Clearly both of them were waiting for the other...

After a long pause, they both replied,
"We're married!"

TEN

Katie concentrated on moving the needle through the deep purple fabric that Freida had chosen for her dress. Across from her, Freida was putting the finishing touches on the hem of her own dress.

She could hardly believe that the wedding was only one day away. Even more difficult to believe was how much they still had to do if they intended to be ready.

The entire time they had been working,

Freida's *mamm* had walked in and out of the large sitting room, checking on their progress and asking Freida about one detail or another.

With so many questions, Katie expected Freida's smile to falter, but it looked like she was smiling more widely now that she had when Katie had begun sewing.

It was a *gut* thing to see her *freind* so *froh* all the time.

And Freida deserves some happiness. She works so hard and she is always there for me.

"*Ach*, Katie. One more day. . . just one more day and I'll be married to Thomas. I don't even care anymore if everything gets done on time. I just want to be married and done with all the details and planning."

"I know you do, Freida. I am so *froh*—so happy—for you." Katie stopped, wanting to say more, but suddenly she felt sad.

When will it be my turn?

* * *

"Have you noticed something, Katie?"

"What's that?"

Freida moved in a bit closer to Katie before continuing, "We were so certain that Mrs. Mueller would find out everything there is to know about Bella—and then the whole town would know in no time."

"*Jah?*"

"Well, here it is almost a week that she's been in town and I've not heard one thing."

"You are absolutely right, Freida."

A minute later, Katie added, with a shrug. "Maybe there is nothing to know. Maybe she really is just a young *maedel* whose life did not go as planned and she wanted to get away and start over."

"But could it truly be that simple? I cannot think of many *Englischers* whose lives are truly that simple, can you?"

Katie thought about it for a minute. Why, even their boss's life was not so simple. *Especially since she went on that cruise.*

"*Nee*, I was expecting to hear more, too."

It had been bugging her and Freida ever

since Mr. O'Neal and Mrs. Simpkins. . .

I suppose I should start thinking of her as Mrs. O'Neal now.

The thought came to her suddenly, and left her unexpectedly feeling very odd about the whole thing.

Ever since they had made their big announcement, Freida and Katie had tried to get the whole story out of them, but all either of them would say was that Mr. O'Neal had shown up unexpectedly on the cruise and had *"swept Miss Amelia off her feet"*.

"Perhaps Mrs. Mueller is losing her touch."

Freida's whispered words made Katie want to laugh, but when she really thought about what her *freind* said, it sort of made sense. It was strange indeed to think so, but there was no denying the fact that no one in town knew anything more about Bella Stanton than they had when she arrived. Even more unusual, no one in town had heard anything more about the cafe owner's and the bakery owner's whirlwind marriage.

They had finally acknowledged their feelings for one another when something happened. . . for weeks they argued, fought and sniped at one another, until they stopped speaking. Six months later, Mrs. Simpkins went on a vacation. A week or so later, without knowing where she was, Mr. O'Neal left. Then they both ended up on the same ship—at the same time—and incredibly, had come back home—together. And were married.

"You could be right, Freida."

"Spooky to think about it, isn't it?"

"You know, it really is." Katie answered, then she stopped to think about it. It really was sort of weird to think that the town's most notorious busybody had managed to miss out on two of the biggest things to happen in their small town since the Sweet Shop had been broken into last year.

Could it get any weirder?

"Katie, did you talk to Travis? Did you

give him all the details?"

"*Jah*, I did. Don't worry, he'll be there."

"I wish we could have asked Bella, but—"

"I talked to Bella. She's coming later with Mrs. Mueller. Everything is arranged."

"I think that covers everything on the list."

"*Jah*. It's all done. Are you ready?"

"I'm ready."

ELEVEN

Travis drove slowly along the road, following the directions Katie had given him the day before, trying desperately not to be distracted by the constant stream of questions that came from the passenger seat.

Gwen was reading the directions and navigating. She had been too excited about coming for him to tell her that he didn't think it would be a good idea. And after his behavior over the last week, he was especially surprised that Freida had even included him in the invitation.

Of course, that could be because she knows I'm driving.

"Oh Travis, aren't weddings just the most exciting thing ever!"

Travis tried not to cringe at the sound of his sister's voice. She was still far too young in his opinion to be so excited about weddings and marriage and romance.

Travis slowed his car as they came upon yet another buggy. The closer they got to Freida's house, the more buggies they passed.

But at least there aren't many cars on these back roads so I can go as slow as I need to.

"Hey, this is cool, huh. We can just follow the buggies. I bet they're all going to the wedding."

Travis looked over at his sister. Why hadn't he thought of that?

"You're absolutely right, Gwen. That will

make it a lot easier to find the place."

With that in mind, he slowed the car and concentrated on following the line of black buggies that was slowly moving along the road in front of them.

After a minute, he managed to match the buggies' speed and noticed that one had taken a place behind him. They had just formed their line around his car.

Amazing people, these Amish.

* * *

Katie watched as Travis followed the long line of buggies that were slowly making their way into Freida's driveway. He stayed right with them, never rushing past or breaking the line, even going so far as to pull into a spot in the yard beside the buggy that had just been in front of him.

She shook her head at the irony of a young man who drove a sports car, following slowly along behind a line of buggies that averaged about ten miles an hour.

How did he even get his car to go that

slow?

She walked towards the car, smiling when Gwen opened her door and rushed out, looking around with a brilliant smile. Katie hurried over then, reaching out to take Gwen's outstretched hand.

"Oh Katie, it's just so exciting."

"It was nice of Freida to invite us." Travis spoke quietly from beside his *schweschder*.

Katie managed to stifle the gasp of surprise, but just barely. She had not heard or seen him move.

"*Jah*, that's our Freida."

She turned toward the house, Gwen's hand still in her own as they moved forward together as a group. "Just so you know, she intended to ask you all along. This is not just because you came to work at the bakery." She spoke to Gwen, but it was Travis who answered.

"That's good to know, isn't it Gwen?"

Gwen made no answer. She was too busy

taking in everything around her. Thinking back to the first wedding she had attended, Katie felt certain her behavior was perfectly normal.

Even young maedels dream of their wedding day.

As a group, they made their way to the barn, where everyone was gathering. Katie was glad to note that the propane heaters were busily putting out heat.

Freida's *mamm* had worried they would not be able to compete with the fierce cold that was typical for November, but they were keeping up nicely.

For sure and for certain, all these bodies are helping, too.

It looked as if Freida and Thomas had invited their entire community—and several others as well. And, as Katie looked around behind them at the crowd, she realized that there were other *Englischer* vehicles pulling into the yard now, too.

There was only one other that she

recognized. It was Mr. O'Neal's car.

Of course Freida would invite them. I am so glad they made it back in time.

"I bet Freida's really excited that Mrs. Simpkins. . . oops. . . I mean Mrs. O'Neal made it in time for the wedding."

Before Katie could respond, Gwen spoke again. "How long do you think it'll take us to get used to that?"

Katie only laughed. Truth be told, she was certain it would take some time for them all. It was such a shock. For six months they had been fighting—and then they just show up married.

"Am I the only one who wants to know more about that?" Travis spoke softly from beside Katie, just as Gwen let go of her hand and rushed over to talk to some young people she must have met at one of the singings she'd attended.

"*Nee,* you are not the only one." She assured him.

"The whole thing is just so unexpected."

"*Jah*, it is." She agreed.

"I mean. . . they seemed to be getting along really great. And then they fought all summer. And they both leave town, then they come back together, and they're married? Something doesn't add up, does it? Am I right?"

Surprised at just how precisely Travis had just restated her own feelings, Katie could only nod in return.

"Oh well, we have plenty of time to find out, right?"

"Hmm." was the only sound that Katie could seem to make.

"They'll have to tell us the whole story sometime."

"*Jah*. . . sometime."

"Right Excuse me, Katie." And then Travis headed across the room to talk to Jake Yoder—and Katie was left standing there looking after him, wondering what had just happened.

He had voiced—almost word for word—

every single one of Katie's thoughts and questions.

Freida was right. It was downright spooky.

Fortunately, someone called out to Katie, and she was forced to turn her attention to other things. She never had the chance to think on it again that day. One person and then another needed her attention—until it was time to stand up by Freida.

Their ceremony was *wunderbaar*—and Freida had never looked more *froh* than she did when the Bishop introduced them to the community as husband and wife.

The rest of the afternoon passed in a blur as seats were shuffled around and tables were brought into the barn to go with the seats and benches.

Only the *Englischers* in attendance stopped to tell Katie how *wunderbaar* the cake tasted, but the looks on the faces of all her neighbors said the same thing to her. Katie was very *froh* she had been able to make Freida's wedding cake. It was one of her gifts to the bride and groom.

It was a *gut* thing to see so many people enjoying the cake, and all of the other treats they had made for the occasion.

* * *

Finally, the wedding dinner was over. The food had been eaten. The gifts had been opened. Tomorrow Freida and Thomas would celebrate their first Thanksgiving as husband and wife. First, they would join her family for an early turkey dinner together. Later in the afternoon, they would join the Yoder family for a late dinner and fellowship.

On Friday, Freida would join her *mamm*, along with several family members in cleaning up everything that had been borrowed for the wedding, then it would all be returned to the rightful owners.

* * *

Katie stood and watched the *froh* couple, accepting well wishes and congratulations from friends and neighbors. As one of

Freida's side sitters, she had been paired at the *eck* with Timothy, Thomas' twin brother. Now people would be teasing her and making comments about what a *wunderbaar* couple they would make.

Katie wasn't interested in Timothy; he seemed happy and content to be single, never paying attention to any particular *maedel*. As for Katie. . . there were one or two *buwes* she had hoped would notice her—until she had met the Davis family. From the moment she had met Travis, she couldn't seem to keep her mind off him.

Travis had spoken to her at Freida's wedding. He had apologized again for being so abrupt with her. Of course, she had assured him that she had forgiven him and it was best forgotten, but she could tell that he still felt badly about the incident.

Katie was trying to be just *freinden* with him, but it was difficult when her emotions ran crazy at times. Her parents wanted her to join the church. She wanted to join the church, which meant she had to let go of her feelings for Travis.

Some days it seemed to be working out okay; other times it seemed impossible! Once she arrived at work, she found herself watching the back door, waiting for him to arrive. Then, when he did come by to pick up the morning or afternoon deliveries, she would get all flustered.

How do I deny my feelings? How do I not? I cannot be baptized and date an Englischer. . .

Dear Gott, what do I do? I am so confused. Is it wrong of me to want what my heart wants?

$$-\!\!-\!\!- \text{EPILOGUE} -\!\!-\!\!-$$

Thanksgiving Day dawned bright and beautiful. Travis was more than a little surprised when he headed towards the kitchen and saw his mother up and about. . . and cooking, Gwen was by her side, peeling potatoes and chattering away about the wedding she had attended the day before.

He stood in the doorway watching for awhile, thinking about how thankful he was to have his family. How grateful he was that his mother was on the mend. How blessed they all were that Mrs. Simpkins had seen goodness in his brothers, instead of criminal tendencies.

I suppose I should start thinking of her as Mrs. O'Neal now.

He smiled as he recalled Katie and Freida —even Gwen—saying that very thing. Yet it was still hard to believe the surprise she and her new husband had dropped on everyone.

Really. . . there are lots to be thankful for.

With a smile on his face, Travis went into the kitchen to join his family. "Good morning ladies. How can I be of help here?" He asked as he moved into the room and wrapped his mother in a gentle hug.

His mother returned the hug before she laughed and waved him away. "Dear boy, there is nothing for you to do right now. Gwen and I have everything covered."

"Later, though, you can help us with the turkey. It's really heavy." Gwen added.

"That's because you're such a little squirt!" Travis teased her.

Gwen swiped at Travis with her spatula as he plucked a piece of cheese off the cutting board on the counter next to her.

"Travis, those are for later." There was indignation in her voice, but she was smiling.

"Son, there is a breakfast casserole that your friend Katie dropped off yesterday that we can have for breakfast. It's very good."

A moment later, Gwen added, "Yeah, you'll want to get some of it before the boys are up. It will disappear fast then. You know how delicious everything is that Katie makes."

Travis did not miss the teasing tone of his sister's voice, even though their mother seemed to be oblivious to it.

So far, this is the only negative part to her new job.

But surely, if Gwen was at the bakery every day, she would see that he and Katie were no more than friends.

If only. . .

That made him think of Katie—and how her feelings seemed to be changing towards him. For awhile, they seemed to be growing closer. Last winter, he drove her to work more often than not.

And helping her decorate the window at Christmas was lots of fun. Then there were the hugs they had shared. He had almost kissed her. He had really wanted to, but he wasn't sure how she would react. He didn't want to spoil things by rushing her.

Lately, she didn't tease him like she used to, even when Freida did. And she was walking to work again. The last time he asked, she had turned him down, saying she needed the exercise.

"Travis, stop daydreaming and come help." Gwen teased.

Pulling on her braids and tweaking her nose, Travis did what she asked. After the turkey was settled in the oven, he watched his sister in the kitchen with his mom. He was more certain than ever that this new job was exactly what she had needed to get her back on the right path.

She was smiling again. She was happy again. She was talking to him again. She was his baby sister again.

And she's home when she's supposed to be now.

* * *

Katie watched as her *bruders* argued playfully over the last helping of casserole. They had *kumme* in from the barn in a *wunderbaar gut* mood and had immediately attacked her breakfast casserole.

As hungry as they all acted, she was a little surprised there was any left for them to fight over. Several times now, she had been sure the next helping would be the last.

The breakfast casserole reminded her that she had dropped one off with Travis' mamm, who was looking much better. Gwen was going to be a gut helper at work, and she could use the knowledge she learned at work to help out at home, too.

Katie looked around the kitchen at her family and felt a sudden wave of thankfulness wash over her. She was immeasurably blessed to have such a *wunderbaar* family.

It was a tremendous blessing to have such a *gut* job at the bakery.

Thinking of the bakery brought her boss to mind.

In all the commotion on Monday, she had never gotten the full story about what had happened to bring about the news that had only been partially shared so far.

There must be an interesting story there. Maybe Travis can ask Sean about it. . . . I wonder if he's having a nice Thanksgiving. . .

HAPPY THANKSGIVING!

... and a time to every purpose under the Heaven.

Ecclesiastes 3:1

RECIPES

Rachel's Pumpkin Pie
Rachel's Sweet Potato Pie
Naomi's Honey Butter
Naomi's Roasted Turkey
Naomi's Holiday Chex Mix
Iva's Cornbread Dressing
Rachel's Pumpkin Bread
Cranberry Pumpkin Bread
Martha's Sausage Balls
Rachel's Sweet Potato Casserole
Pumpkin Pecan Pancakes
Pumpkin Orange Cookies

RACHEL'S PUMPKIN PIE

INGREDIENTS

   2 cups fresh pumpkin

   2 cups evaporated milk

   1/2 cup white sugar

   2 large eggs

   1 teaspoon ground cinnamon

   1/2 teaspoon ground ginger

   1/2 teaspoon ground cloves

   2 9" unbaked pie shells

Cut pumpkin in half and remove seeds. Place on cookie sheet (cut side up). Place in oven. Bake at 325°F for 30-45 minutes. Pumpkin peeling will separate while cooking (and pumpkin will soften). Throw away peel.

Preheat oven to 350°F. Mash pumpkin and then measure out 2 cups. Mix together dry ingredients: sugar, cinnamon, ginger and cloves. Break eggs into small bowl and beat before adding to dry mixture. Stir in fresh pumpkin until well blended. Slowly add evaporated milk (the slower, the better).

Pour into thawed pie shells. Don't over-fill. Bake for 45-50 minutes (or until center is set). Cool on wire racks (it slices easier if you wait until it's cool). Cover and refrigerate any remaining pie.

RACHEL'S SWEET POTATO PIE

INGREDIENTS:

3 cups sweet potatoes

1/2 cup evaporated milk

1 1/4 cups white sugar

2 large eggs, beaten

1/2 cup unsalted butter

2 teaspoons pure vanilla

2 teaspoons real maple syrup

2 9" unbaked pie shells

Preheat oven to 350°F. Peel, slice and boil 3 large or 4 medium sweet potatoes until they are soft enough to mash. In medium bowl, scoop 3 cups mashed potatoes (works best if they're still warm) over butter slices/chunks. Break eggs into small bowl and beat before adding to sweet potatoes. Stir in remaining ingredients one at a time, adding syrup last. Mix thoroughly after each addition.

Pour mixture into thawed pie shells. Bake for 45-50 minutes (or until center is set). Cool on wire racks (it slices easier if you wait until it's cool to cut). Cover and refrigerate any remaining pie.

NAOMI'S HONEY BUTTER

INGREDIENTS:

1 cup unsalted butter (softened)
4 tablespoons honey

Blend thoroughly. Enjoy!

I included this recipe because my family and friends always ask for it.

We enjoy it with biscuits, rolls, cornbread, on toast...

Anything goes!

NAOMI'S ROASTED TURKEY

INGREDIENTS:

1 large frozen turkey

1 giant oval rack roaster (I use a disposable one)

1 turkey size oven bag

1 tablespoon flour

Thaw turkey in refrigerator (1 day for every 4 pounds). When ready to cook turkey, remove neck and giblets. Wash turkey thoroughly in cold water. Pat dry. Shake flour in oven bag to coat. Place turkey in oven bag. Close with nylon tie. Cut several slits in top of bag. Place bag in oval rack roaster. Tuck sides of bag in pan.

Bake at 350°F (time will be determined by weight).Bake a 12# turkey for 2 hours, bake a 20# turkey for 2 1/2 hours. When done, cut open bag, remove turkey and broth. I usually have several cups of broth to use in gravy, soups, etc. Slice and serve. Pan can be re-used several times.

This is a very simple way to roast a turkey, but many friends and readers ask how I roast my turkey, so I want to include it here for Thanksgiving.

Following the simple directions above, my turkey always turns out tender, moist, and delicious!

I don't have a roaster, so I buy an aluminum throw-away pan and oven bags each year. We roast the turkey, then fix several pans of chex mix... then roast another turkey at Christmas, make more chex mix... and toss the pan.

NAOMI'S HOLIDAY CHEX MIX

INGREDIENTS:

    3 cups rice cereal

    3 cups corn cereal

    3 cups wheat cereal

    1 1/2 cups pretzels

    1 1/2 cups bugles

I mix it up, depending on whatever I have on hand. I'll add 1 cup of pretzels, then add 2 more cups of a variety of stuff... bugles, nuts, cheese-its, Ritz crackers, Cheerios, and/or goldfish crackers (just be sure to have 12 cups total). Mix all this in a large bowl.

SEASONING:

    6 tablespoons unsalted butter, melted

    3 tablespoons Worcestershire sauce

    1 1/2 teaspoons seasoned salt

    3/4 teaspoon garlic powder

1/2 teaspoon onion powder

Mix these in a small bowl, then pour carefully over cereal mixture. Bake at 250°F for 1 hour, turning every 15 minutes with a spatula or big wooden spoon.

Store in airtight container.

Enjoy!

IVA'S CORNBREAD DRESSING

STEP 1:

    3 cups cornmeal

    1 large egg

    1/2 celery stalk

    1 medium onion

    * milk

Preheat oven to 450°F. Dice celery and onion. Mix together cornmeal, egg, and the diced celery and onion. Add enough milk to make a thin or loose batter. Bake in iron skillet for 25 minutes or until done. Let set overnight.

STEP 2:

    2 large eggs

    1 stick of unsalted butter

    3 teaspoons sage

    * chicken broth

* chicken pieces, cooked

* salt (to taste)

* pepper (to taste)

Preheat oven to 400°F. Chop cornmeal into pieces. Combine eggs, butter, sage, salt, and pepper. Add cornbread, chicken pieces and enough chicken broth to a stirring consistency.

Pour dressing into large baking dish. Bake for 30-40 minutes or until firm.

RACHEL'S PUMPKIN BREAD

INGREDIENTS:

1 1/2 cups white sugar

4 large eggs

6 tablespoons unsalted butter

15 ounce can pure pumpkin

3/4 cup whole milk

3 1/2 cups all-purpose flour

1 teaspoon baking powder

1 teaspoon baking soda

1 teaspoon salt

2 teaspoons cinnamon

1/2 teaspoon nutmeg

1/4 teaspoon ginger

1/4 teaspoon cloves

1 1/2 cups pecans, chopped

Preheat oven to 350°F. Grease and flour 2 loaf pans. Cream together sugar and butter until smooth. Add eggs and beat until light and fluffy. Add pumpkin and milk.

Stir together flour, baking powder, baking soda, salt, spices and pecans. Combine dry ingredients and pumpkin mixture; stir until ingredients are moistened. Pour into loaf pans. Tap on counter to settle dough.

Bake for 55-60 minutes (or until center is set). Cool on wire racks for 5-10 minutes. Turn out onto rack to finish cooling. Brush melted butter over tops of pumpkin bread. Wrap in plastic wrap to retain freshness.

You can also bake this bread in small, individual size loaf pans (bake for 45 minutes). These are great idea for gifts.

CRANBERRY PUMPKIN BREAD

INGREDIENTS:

2 1/4 cups all-purpose flour

1 1/2 cups white sugar

2 large eggs

1/2 cup cranberries (fresh, frozen, or dried)

6 tablespoons unsalted butter

1 3/4 cups pure pumpkin

2 teaspoons baking powder

1/2 teaspoon salt

2 teaspoons cinnamon

1/2 teaspoon nutmeg

1/4 teaspoon ginger

1/4 teaspoon cloves

Preheat oven to 350°F. Grease and flour 2 loaf pans. Combine flour, baking powder, salt, and spices. Cream together sugar, eggs, butter and pumpkin until smooth. Add pumpkin mixture to flour mixture; stir until moistened. Fold in cranberries. Pour batter into prepared loaf pans. Tap on counter to settle dough.

Bake for 55-60 minutes (or until center is set). Cool on wire racks for 5-10 minutes. Turn out onto rack to finish cooling. Brush melted butter over tops of pumpkin bread. Wrap in plastic wrap to retain freshness.

You can also bake this bread in small, individual size loaf pans (bake for 45 minutes). These are great idea for gifts.

MARTHA'S SAUSAGE BALLS

INGREDIENTS:

2 pounds regular sausage

1 1/4 cups all-purpose baking mix

4 cups cheddar cheese, shredded

1/4 cup finely chopped onion

1/4 cup finely chopped celery

1/4 cup garlic powder

Preheat oven to 350°F. Finely chop onion and celery. Mix all ingredients together and form into balls.

Bake for 15 minutes on ungreased cookie sheet until golden brown.

These simple treats can be prepared ahead of time during special events. Mix the ingredients together and form into balls, then freeze. When ready, thaw for 30 minutes, bake and enjoy!

RACHEL'S SWEET POTATO CASSEROLE

INGREDIENTS:

1 1/2 cups sweet potatoes

1/4 cup brown sugar

1/4 cup orange juice

1 large egg, beaten

1/4 cup unsalted butter, melted

1 teaspoon pure vanilla

1 teaspoon ground cinnamon

1/4 teaspoon ground nutmeg

1 teaspoon real maple syrup

3 cups miniature marshmallows

Preheat oven to 350°F. Peel, slice and boil 2-3 medium sweet potatoes until they are soft enough to mash. In medium bowl, scoop 1 1/2 cups mashed potatoes (works best if they're still warm) over butter slices/chunks. Break egg into small bowl and beat before adding to sweet potatoes. Stir in remaining ingredients one at a time, adding syrup last. Mix thoroughly after each addition.

Pour mixture into large baking dish. Bake for 18-20 minutes. Top with marshmallows and continue to bake until marshmallows are lightly browned.

If you don't have time to prepare sweet potatoes, you can substitute with canned yams, although the taste won't be quite as good.

PUMPKIN PECAN PANCAKES

INGREDIENTS:

1 1/2 cups all-purpose flour

1 teaspoon baking powder

1/2 teaspoon salt

1 large egg

1 cup whole milk

1/2 cup pure pumpkin

2 tablespoons white sugar

1/4 teaspoon ground cinnamon

* pinch of ground nutmeg

* pinch of ground ginger

1 cup pecans, chopped

* butter or oil (for cooking)

Combine all of the ingredients except pecans and butter; stir until blended. Lightly butter hot griddle and pour 1/4 cup batter for each pancake. Sprinkle with chopped pecans. When bubbles break around the edges, it's time to flip pancake over. Cook until brown on each side. Serve hot with syrup of your choice.

PUMPKIN ORANGE COOKIES

STEP 1

2 1/2 cups all-purpose flour

1/2 teaspoon baking soda

1/2 teaspoon salt

1/2 cup brown sugar

1 cup white sugar

1 cup unsalted butter

1 large egg

24 ounces pure pumpkin

2 tablespoons orange juice

1 teaspoon orange peel, grated

Preheat oven to 375°F. Combine flour, baking soda and salt in a bowl. Cream white sugar, brown sugar and butter in a large mixing bowl. Add pumpkin, orange juice, orange peel and egg to sugar mixture; beat for 2 minutes. Drop rounded spoonfuls of dough onto an ungreased cookie sheet.

Bake for 12-14 minutes. Remove from oven and transfer cookies to wire racks to cool.

STEP 2:

1 1/2 cups confectioners sugar

2-3 tablespoons orange juice

1/2 teaspoon orange peel, grated

Combine ingredients in a medium bowl and beat until smooth. Drizzle over cookies. Be sure to allow time for icing to harden before serving.

TURN THE PAGE
FOR EXCLUSIVE
BONUS CONTENT

DISCUSSION QUESTIONS

WARNING : SPOILERS AHEAD!

1) Freida and Thomas are preparing to marry. How important is it to be emotionally and responsibly prepared? Do you think sometimes people make the wedding seem more important that the marriage?

2) Mrs. Simpkins has left on vacation... Does it seem more like she's running away from Mr. O'Neal? Should they quit talking or try to work out their problems? What would you do in their situation?

3) Katie and Freida are over-worked. Their friend tells them they should hire more help. Do you

think this is a good solution? Why did you think

Mrs. Simpkins not hire more help before leaving?

4) Sean is also over-worked after Mr. O'Neal

leaves. What should he do? Is it a good solution to

have Travis help out or should he hire more help?

What would you do in this situation?

5) Gwen starts helping out at the bakery. Do you

feel she's too young for so much responsibility? Do

you think this will help her gain maturity or

perhaps grow up too fast? How could this help or

harm her relationship with her family?

6) Amelia and Andrew return home together. And

they're married. Do you think they married in

haste? If they still have doubts or problems, could

this hurt their marriage? How should they go

about working things out?

7) In the last book, Katie decided she wants to join

the church and marry someone who belongs to the

church. Do you think she's making the right choice? Or should she give Travis another chance? Which do you think will make her happier?

AUTHOR INTERVIEW

Q: What was your inspiration for writing Pumpkin Pie Mystery?

A: Thanksgiving is one of my most favorite times. I wanted to share this holiday with my readers. What better way than to celebrate two marriages and to visit everyone in our beloved Abbott Creek community.

Q: What do you hope your readers will take away from reading Pumpkin Pie Mystery—or others in the series?

A: That by working together (and trusting God), our problems can be worked out.

Q: Will there be more books in the Amish Sweet Shop Mystery series?

A: Oh, yes. I'm working on book five now, titled Chocolate Truffle Mystery, which I hope will be released next year.

Q: What does your home look like?

A: My home is slowly taking on a holiday look... I have my Christmas tree up, so decorating can be done the week of Thanksgiving. This year we're putting up outdoor lights and decorations, too. . . to share the joy of Christmas with others.

Q: What is another favorite Bible verse and why?

A: Below is another one of my favorites. . .

"And be ye kind one to another, tenderhearted, forgiving one another, even as God for Christ's sake hath forgiven you." ~Ephesians 4:32

Q: Do you have a favorite scene in your newest release?

A: My favorite scene is when Amelia and Andrew return. . . and surprise the girls.

ACKNOWLEDGMENTS

To God be the glory! I have been having a rough year and several times thought I wouldn't be able to finish this story, but God (and my daughter) gave me the strength and courage to continue!

When God placed it on my heart to write a light-hearted mystery series, I'm glad I obeyed.

Thanks to my daughter Rachel, who not only designs my covers, but helped me finish my book on time. Rachel, I couldn't have done it without you!

A big thank you goes out to Pam, our dear friend and the founder of S&G Publishing. She continues to inspire me. . .

Thank you to my awesome beta readers, who worked so hard to meet my tight deadline with this book. . . you guys rock!

Last, but by no means least, thank you to my awesome readers, who do so much to encourage me and continue to make this series a huge success!

ABOUT THE AUTHOR

Naomi Miller mixes up a batch of intrigue, sprinkled with Amish, Mennonite, and English characters, adding a pinch of mystery, and a dash of romance!

Naomi's days are spent focusing on her writing, editing and homeschooling her grandchildren. She loves her new career as an author, blogger and inspirational speaker.

She schedules several book events each year and enjoys the opportunity to meet readers face-to-face. When she's not rushing to meet a deadline, Naomi loves to make time to attend writing conferences, workshops, and other author events.

She is a member of the American Christian Fiction Writers organization (ACFW), the Knoxville and the Authors Guild of Tennessee (AGT).

Whenever time permits, Naomi can be found in one of two favorite places. . . the beach and the mountains.

Naomi loves traveling with her family, singing inspirational/gospel music, taking daily walks, and witnessing to others of the amazing grace of Jesus Christ.

AUTHOR LINKS

WEBSITE: https://naomimillerauthor.com

NEWSLETTER SIGN UP: http://eepurl.com/bPdjGn

FACEBOOK:
https://www.facebook.com/NaomiMillerAuthor

INSTAGRAM: https://twitter.com/AuthorNaomi

PINTEREST: http://www.pinterest.com/authornaomi

GOODREADS:
https://www.goodreads.com/NaomiMiller

BOOKBUB: https://www.bookbub.com/authors/naomi-miller

INDIEBOUND: http://bit.ly/1PsB9MR

FICTION FINDER: http://bit.ly/1UOlI5P

DON'T MISS THE NEXT BOOK IN THIS SERIES

Chocolate Truffle Mystery

———————— ONE ————————

Monday morning began just like any other Monday—with one exception. Valentine's Day was two days away and there was much to be done if the Sweet Shop was to be ready on time.

Over the past two weeks, Katie Chupp, with the help of her co-worker Gwen Davis, had been baking more and more special treats for the upcoming holiday, most of which were quickly snapped up by the residents of Abbott Creek.

Orders had been coming in for cookies, cakes, and candies. There were almost as many orders as they had prepared for Christmas. Katie was especially thankful that she had a willing—and helpful—assistant.

Danki Gott, for bringing the Davis family to our community. Gwen is such a blessing to me. I don't know what I would have done the past couple of months without her help. Please bless her family with gut health, supply their needs, and keep them safe.

Only a moment or two after Katie had finished her prayer and went back to work, Travis Davis opened the back door and walked in.

"Hiya, Katie-girl. Hey, Gwennie."

"*Gudemariye*, Travis."

"Hey, big brother. I'm almost ready to go."

"Good. You don't want to be late to school," he teased his younger sister. "Katie, I'll come back to pick up the morning deliveries after I drop off Gwen. See ya in a bit."

"*Allrecht.*"

After Travis and Gwen left, Katie went back over the list of supplies she would need to fill the orders for the next few days. Then she double-checked the customer orders that still needed to be filled.

Katie turned at the sound of the swinging double doors, followed by her newest co-worker's voice.

"*Appeditlich* treats for families and friends. I love selling all these delicious treats!" Bella was practically dancing as she pushed through the swinging doors to the kitchen.

Katie smiled at Bella's use of the Pennsylvania Dutch. Many of her plain neighbors would just shake their heads when *Englischers* used their words, but Katie thought it was sweet that Bella was taking the time to listen and learn—and most importantly, using them correctly around Katie.

Bella Stanton had moved to their small community a few days before Thanksgiving. She had applied for a job at the bakery almost immediately and to Katie's delight, was dependable and a hard worker.

"*Gudemariye*, Bella. I hope you had a *gut* weekend. Did you get some rest yesterday?"

"Yes, I actually rested most of the day. For some reason I was more tired than usual."

Katie frowned thoughtfully at Bella's

comment. "I still think it would be a *gut* idea for you to make an appointment with a doctor. You think I didn't see how long it took you to get over that stomach bug you had, but I did."

Katie had been meaning to talk to Bella about her health, but had put it off during the holidays. Then in January, Bella had asked for time off. When she returned, she seemed to avoid everyone. Katie was more than a bit worried about her.

"Bella, please. We need to have a chat. Although you keep telling me you are *allrecht,* there have been many times it was all I could do to not send you home to lie down. By Christmas you seemed to feel better, but you still seem to tire so easily. I really think you should see a doctor."

"Well," Bella looked down as she spoke, not meeting Katie's eyes. "I probably should have shared with you that I saw a doctor last month when I visited my parents. Everything is fine. I feel better than I have in a long time." She turned away then suddenly.

"Do you think I should make more coffee? We've already had more customers today than usual." Without waiting for an answer, she went on quickly. "Yes, I'm going to make more coffee." And before Katie could comment, she was heading for the storeroom.

Katie watched the door, waiting for her to emerge while thinking about how, when the bakery had opened only a few short years ago, they had not offered drinks, but so many customers had requested coffee, Mrs. O'Neal had finally made it available, as well as individual bottles of water and juice.

When Bella emerged, she did not give Katie a chance to say anything, moving quickly through the kitchen and then on to the front of the bakery. The double doors swayed silently a moment before coming to rest.

Katie watched for a moment, thinking over what had just happened. She had been worrying for some time now—and it was clear that Bella had no intention of talking with her about those concerns.

When she had *kumme* to work in November, Katie had been grateful for the help, but hesitant about becoming too attached to the young woman—especially since Bella had requested several days off just after the new year. When she had learned that Bella left town, Katie wondered if she would return—or simply go back to wherever she had come from. And Katie had hoped she would return, but resigned herself to losing a *gut* worker.

When she asked Ada Mueller, the woman had simply stated that Bella was off visiting family. Nothing else was said.

Which was another odd thing about the situation. Mrs. Mueller had always been considered the town gossip; she could ferret out details on what was going on with people faster than anyone else.

Mrs. Mueller had been coming into the bakery for years. She would buy a cup of *kaffe* and a danish. Every day she'd sit at the same table for an hour or so. And when her *freinden* came in, they'd stop, sit down and chat awhile.

Katie wasn't certain when it had stopped, but it seemed to be just after Thanksgiving. Most mornings Mrs. Mueller still came by for *kaffe* and a danish, but she rarely sat down at a table unless there were no other customers around. Whenever one of her *freinden* came in, if she was sitting at a table, she would greet them, but after a minute or two, she would leave.

Katie couldn't remember the last time she had heard Mrs. Mueller gossiping about anyone.

I wonder what could have happened to her. . . I do hope no one was unkind to her, although that seems unlikely. She doesn't even chat much with Bella when she comes by, although Bella is still renting a room from her. Perhaps they eat dinner together and that is when they do their chatting.

Still, it seemed strange that Mrs. Mueller had changed so much. Sometimes it seemed like she was avoiding people. *What on earth could have happened to cause such a thing?*

When Bella had returned to Abbott Creek, she'd looked even more troubled than when she had first showed up in town, although she seemed *froh* to be back.

Katie had wanted to ask Bella about her trip, but didn't want to appear nosy. And for a time after her return, Bella seemed aloof and distant, though only a very short time. Since then, she had been happier and more friendly each day.

Dear Gott, please bless Mrs. Mueller and Bella. Keep them both safe. If something has happened to Mrs. Mueller, please protect her and help her to be a blessing to those around her. And whatever Bella's reason for moving here, I pray you will guide her and help me to be a freind to her.

DON'T MISS BOOK ONE:

MORE BOOKS FROM NAOMI

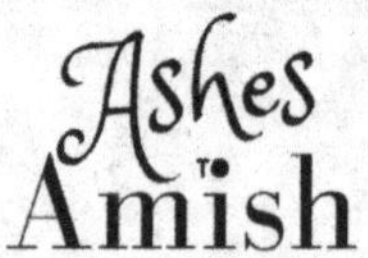

What if the little Cinder girl had been Amish...

Fix dinner, Ella. Clean the House, Ella. Get the shoes fixed, Ella.

Ella is different than most young women in town. She would rather read than watch television. She values kindness over popularity, and she secretly wishes for a family who actually wants her around.

Was it a curse... or a blessing that left Aden Bontrager scarred for life...

After the horrific accident that claimed the life of his fiance, the last thing Aden wants to deal with is the much too appealing new schoolteacher who never really fit anywhere... until she and her father moved to the small town that lost so much on the same night Aden turned into a bit of a beast.

Amelia Simpkins may be a great cook, and have a head for business, but sweet treats are out of her league and the owner of the Irish Blessings Cafe says it's because she adds the tart to the Sweet Shop's new dessert that Katie Chupp insists is only filled with lemony goodness.

The two shop owners' constant bickering sends sparks flying through Abbott Creek's usual calm... and when Andrew's cafe suffers from some rather unusual pest problems, the town starts taking sides.

It's the time of year when the residents of Abbott Creek give thanks for their blessings.

But Katie is having difficulty deciding whether she should be thankful. . . or careful of the new relationships she has developed over the previous year...

Katie Chupp is not the only person in Abbott Creek looking forward to the most romantic holiday of the year...

But Valentine's Day will not be all hearts and flowers. There are secrets to be kept, feelings to be explored, and difficult decisions to be made — and each one has something to do with the heart.

Will those secrets come between friends? Will the happy couples in Abbott Creek get to celebrate. . . together?

Between babies and budding romances, busy schedules and unexpected gossip, the small town and its residents may never be the same.

Everyone at the Sweet Shop Bakery and the Irish Blessings cafe is worrying over Bella and her baby – and busily trying to convince her to take it easy.

Katie is not the only person in town with some big decisions ahead of her. And the busy summer season is kicked off with a big surprise for everyone.

Will Leah Fisher find love because of a buggy accident?

Could love soften her heart so that she is able to see her answered prayers in Naomi Yoder or will she drive a wedge between her father and the only woman he has shown interest in since Elisabeth Fisher's death?

After their parents marry, the Fisher kids must find a place within the family for Rebekah, who is not at all used to such chaos – having grown up with a father who was ill most of her life, a mother who spent her days taking care of a sick husband and grandparents who doted on her to the point where she felt more like their daughter than their grand-daughter.

SOPHIE IS A KITTEN WHO FOUND TWO CHILDREN . . . AND DECIDED TO ADOPT THEM AS HER OWN

Read along with Sammy and Macy as they tell the story of finding a little lost kitten, naming her, loving her, and making her part of their (or rather, becoming her own) family.

Enjoy Thanksgiving with them. Read about how Sophie celebrates this fun holiday filled with food, family and mischief.

Then read about how Sophie's family made the move from the big city... and Sophie followed.

Now she has her own house, a big yard, and new kitty friends right next door!

MORE FROM

S&G PUBLISHING

WELCOME TO SILVER CITY: WHERE HAPPILY EVER AFTER IS STILL A MODERN GIRL'S DREAM!

Meet Cindy, a soft-spoken maid-in-training who secretly wishes she could do a little more than clean the prince's toilets...

As good as orphaned, Cindy works for her step-mother, who owns a high class maid service that caters to the well-to-do families of Silver City.

BOOK ONE OF THE SILVER CITY PRINCESS STORIES

WELCOME TO SILVER CITY: WHERE HAPPILY EVER AFTER IS STILL A MODERN GIRL'S DREAM!

Maree is not your average girl. She rides, climbs trees, is an expert archer, and a constant embarrassment to her very proper mother.

If only she could have been born a boy... like her three rambunctious younger brothers... who can do no wrong in their parents' eyes...

BOOK TWO OF THE SILVER CITY PRINCESS STORIES

www.ingramcontent.com/pod-product-compliance
Lightning Source LLC
Chambersburg PA
CBHW011139190726
48289CB00012B/3082